Her Fake Blitz

Houston Heights-Book 2

Gia Stone

Her Fake Blitz
Houston Heights- Book 2
Copyright © 2024 Gia Stone
All rights reserved.

ISBN: (ebook) 978-1-964636-01-6
(print) 978-1-964636-02-3

Inkspell Publishing
207 Moonglow Circle #101
Murrells Inlet, SC 29576

Edited By Toni Kelley
Cover art By Emily's World By Design

DEDICATION

This book is dedicated to the calorie counters, the self-doubters, and those who achieved their dreams despite it all.

CHAPTER ONE

This was going to be easy. Easier than her SAT's, which she aced. Alex blew the hair from her face. A locker room interview. This player was well-known for being an ass. But it didn't matter. Alex had been given an exclusive pre-season interview with Cane Clayburn, the starting Quarterback for the Texans. He was finally back after several rounds of surgery on his shoulder. Would he even know the difference if she asked him an off the record question? Probably not. The guy had idiot metaphorically written on his face. From his blue eyes that held no distinguishable thoughts behind them to the smile that was always present on his face. It was obvious he had a simple mind.

Alex pushed through the door of the locker room. The man waiting behind the door was built like a muscular machine but Alex was determined to hold her own. She was above average height for a woman. A good three inches above. She was proud of her five feet eight inches. In school it had been a sore spot when she had stuck out in class pictures, now she held her head high. Being tall was powerful. She liked being able to reach all the items on the grocery store shelves. Being able to reach things in her kitchen without a stool. In comparison, her friend, Vanessa had to get a stool and still couldn't reach into the back of the cabinet unless she climbed onto the counter. She reminded Alex of a little gnome.

Alex had specifically chosen to wear her three-inch heels for today's interview. The taller she could be in this room full of male testosterone the better. Being around athletes her entire life had given her an insider's sense of knowledge of how things worked on and off the field. She could cite players stats such as height, weight, and everything that would be important to compare against other players. But she also knew what their weaknesses were. Their tells of uncomfortableness. How they would respond to questions that deflated their egos. One would think these athletes would always be pumped but underneath their sweaty uniforms and thick pads lay a little bit of insecurity. Alex knew how to pick at that when she needed to.

Cane Clayburn was six-foot-seven-inches, almost exactly a foot taller than Alex. Even in her heels he towered over her. His head reached the top of the lockers. He could, without a doubt, touch the ceiling effortlessly. This was insignificant to Alex. She was there for a quote and to do a follow-up report from her first article about his shortcomings of the previous season. She was not interested in his height or any of his other inconsequential musings he normally spewed from his sideline interviews.

He had his back turned to her. His muscular shoulders bare other than a few drops of water that cascaded down the remainder of his back. A white towel hung low on his hips. Alex gasped. Her face warmed.

Cane turned around and flashed a big smile, displaying bright white teeth. He probably had them bleached. He seemed like the kind of guy that thought highly of his appearance. "Huh. I thought you were a guy."

Alex pressed her lips together. "Nope, all lady parts over here." Typical. Of course he assumed she was a man. He couldn't form a thought large enough to consider the name Alex might belong to a woman or that a woman could be a sports reporter. She rolled her eyes. Such a clown.

She had pre-planned this interview. She had to. It was imperative for her to be one hundred and ten percent prepared. For this interview, she knew she had to come in strong but smooth like honey to get him to talk. She needed quotes that were better than his sideline one liners that were always retweeted by millions. She wanted something better. She wanted to show him for what he truly was. Her mission was clear. Get a few soundbites and a quote that would no doubt be all over Monday morning's paper.

"You looked great out there today. How is your shoulder feeling?"

"Really good, you want to feel it for yourself?" Cane flexed his bicep into a large boulder of muscles and nodded at his own perfection. His eyes sparkled. A clear indication he wanted her to enjoy his physical splendor.

"That's actually your bicep. Your shoulder is a little bit higher." She pointed to her own shoulder and demonstrated the exact spot of where his surgery would have been. Alex had done her research on the implications of a separated shoulder and what type of training and physical therapy would be required for Cane to return to the field. Houston is a medical mecca for the world and Cane had received top-notch treatment. His team's fate rested upon those taut muscles. The team was on track to achieve Super Bowl rings this year. That is, if Cane's shoulder held up.

Cane laughed. "Ha, that's right. I had almost forgotten about your previously entertaining article. Though, next time you might want to do a better job with your back story."

Alex raised an eyebrow at him. Yes, her article had not exactly been full of flattery but there was nothing about it that wasn't thoroughly researched. Investigation was her forte.

"I'm glad you were entertained. Did someone have to read it to you? My articles aren't meant for an eighth-grade education." Her eyes focused on his face. No need to get distracted by his physique.

"Funny enough, I was able to get through each one of your four syllable words. What were there, three of them? Maybe add a bit more variety next time. You used the word arbitrary twice. Isn't that a writer faux pas?"

Alex bit her lip. *Don't say anything more. Just ask your questions and get the hell out of here.* The air in the room felt much too hot and it was not due to Cane and all his bare muscles. No, it was the anger that radiated through her. There was no way he was going to get her goat. Absolutely not. She was a professional.

"Hmm…speaking of fauxpas. I noticed you weren't quite able to get any balls in the end zone tonight. How are you feeling about the game next week?"

Cane's eyes dropped for a sliver of a second. If Alex wasn't a keen interviewer, she might have missed it.

"I'm feeling great about the game and about getting my balls to the end zone." He popped his knuckles. It was his tell. Alex had watched enough interviews with Cane to know when he got frustrated, he would fiddle with his hands. Good. This was the perfect moment to get the soundbites she needed.

"What's the back-up plan if you are unsuccessful? Will they pull you in the first quarter or let you try for five minutes of the second quarter before subbing Bronson in?"

Cane laughed. "Sweetheart, I'll be playing the whole game."

Alex smiled. If there was one thing she despised most, it was being called *sweetheart* during an interview. It wasn't enough that so many players didn't give her the same respect they gave male reporters but calling her 'sweetheart' was her point of no return. It was time to stick the knife in deeper. She would need to catch him off guard to make him slip-up. Just like when he'd had his eyes on the tight end and didn't see the play from the outside linebacker. Like the one that had taken him out of the game last season.

"I noticed as you made that last throw your elbow

paused for a second. Was that a mental pause caused by fear or did something physical inside your arm cause the delay?"

Cane's lips formed two solid lines. He scratched his head for a moment. Obviously, he needed to find something to say. His brain most likely only had a few prepared responses and Alex had asked a question he wasn't ready for.

He took a deep breath. "I don't ever have fear when I'm on the field. Fear doesn't enter my frame of mind when I walk into this stadium or any other stadium I'm about to play in. Fear is something that runs deeper than the points on a scoreboard. But to answer your question about my elbow, you're right, there was a bit of a pause. Sometimes that happens in life." He rubbed his lips together. "Sometimes everything seems like all systems are go and then you realize you are standing in a male locker room in three-inch heels and you couldn't be more out of place. So, you take a deep breath and retreat to your house, put on your yoga pants, grab a bowl of ice cream and watch some Real Housewives show. That's where you feel comfortable. That's the kind of moment when your elbow doesn't pause." He raised his eyebrows at her, confident he had struck a nerve.

It took every ounce of Alex's self-control not to slap him or worse...cry. He had no idea what it was like being a female sports reporter. She did belong. Maybe not in a male locker room, but that had been his choice. His stipulations were that the interview take place in the locker room and not on the field.

And he was wrong. Alex wouldn't be caught dead watching a Real Housewives show. She would rather slit her own wrists than view the utter verbal diarrhea and superficial variety that showed up week after week on those poorly scripted reality programs.

"Well, I think I've got all the information I need. Thanks for your time." Alex turned on her heel and stormed out of the locker room. She didn't care if the Texans won the Super Bowl. This would be the last time she ever interviewed Cane

Clayburn. She would write her article for tomorrow. If he didn't like the article she had previously written, he was in for a big surprise with the words she would dole out for Monday's paper.

"Cane Clayburn, America's corn-fed farming son is returning to the big leagues this football season. With so much pressure on his shoulders will his brain be able to keep up with all the plays for the Houston Texans?

When asked how his shoulder was feeling, Clayburn responded that he was confident about his scheduled performance next Sunday then rubbed his bicep and stated it felt great. Perhaps, the Texans might want to add anatomy to the sideline discussion, just in case any other body parts are mentioned to Cane. Surely, they don't want to confuse the man any further.

He might have majored in business at the University of Texas but let's hope it had nothing to do with the business of the body. Clearly an additional course would be needed in regard to physical locations for Clayburn. How is he even able to run a play? Do the Texans have to use a color chart or maybe they work with hand signs for him.

Despite his lack of knowledge regarding anatomy, his sunny disposition makes up for it. Cane admits that where he feels most comfortable is in a pair of "yoga pants with a bowl of ice cream watching some Real Housewives show."

It will be interesting to see whether Cane's shoulder holds up this season or if he retreats to the comforts of his home cuddled up with some Blue Bell."

CHAPTER TWO

Cane pulled up the article on his phone again and laughed. Dang that girl had sass. He didn't bother knocking on the door to Alex's office. He would much rather catch her off guard. The secretary downstairs had offered to walk him up and show him to Alex's office. She was cute, not as cute as Alex but cute enough. Six months ago, Cane would have asked for the secretary's phone number, he might have even used it. But he was done messing around. He'd had his fun but his injury had put things in perspective. He wasn't getting any younger. He needed to quit wasting time chasing strange.

Chasing sass was another thing entirely.

"Hello, sweetheart. I can see from the look on your face you weren't expecting me," Cane drawled. The annoyance that flashed on her face was worth the drive over in rush hour traffic.

Alex's eyes widened and her full lips fell into a perfect O. She was cute, not modelesque like he was used to. She was that cliché girl next door that everyone was supposed to be so excited about. Cane had never had a preference. It was more about a pulse and curves. Lock in and then move on. Her dark brown hair was tied in a knot at the top of her head, a pencil stuck through it to keep it anchored. She was wearing black-framed glasses which gave her just enough of the sexy librarian vibe to be hot. He had never been one for that fantasy, but why not? Time was of the essence and there was something about Alex that kept him in suspense. Kept him in the need to want more. To explore. His curiosity had been ignited and he wasn't sure if it was about her insistence to try and embarrass him or if there was something more.

He glanced down at the picture on her desk: the football team at University of Oklahoma. Alex was standing beside the coach smiling. Of course, she was an OU fan. Maybe that is why she had it out for him. In college he'd played for their rival, UT.

"See you got the flowers I sent. Great article by the way. You're still shit at research but you nailed the humor so I'll give you a pass." He nodded to the vase on her desk. He ordered three dozen red and white roses tied off with a blue ribbon: Texan colors. He didn't sign the card. She would know they were from him.

Alex stiffened in her chair, visibly riled. Pink crept up her neck and settled on her cheeks. Alex stood up and walked around to the front of her desk. She straightened her back so she was standing at her full height. She was trying to look taller which was comical because Cane dwarfed her. He had a good foot in height and more than a hundred pounds on her. Standing up straight didn't change shit about that.

"Of course you would send me flowers and address them to Ms. Lady Parts Reporter."

"Of course," he agreed. "You seemed pretty proud of your lady parts. Almost like you wanted to show me."

There was a flash of a smile but it was gone as quickly as it had appeared. "I can't accept gifts from players over fifty dollars."

"Well then that's a shame cause this one is way over that price. But I won't tell anyone if you don't. It almost came under until I went and signed it. Damn my celebrity upping the value of things." His mouth hitched up in a lazy smile as he handed her a wrapped package.

Alex eyed the box suspiciously. "What's that?"

"Something you're needing. And you're welcome."

Alex tore off the paper and examined the hardbound thesaurus. She smiled and shook her head. "Look at you, Corn Fed, you realized *thesaurus* wasn't the name of a dinosaur." Alex tossed it on her desk without bothering to read the inscription.

Cane laughed. "You like your big words but you use the same ones over and over. Shake it up a bit, Ms. Lady Parts."

"Look at you, reading and everything. Or did you have someone read you the article, too?"

"Read it all by myself. Seems to me you went to a whole lot of effort just to see me. If you want to go out with me, Alex, just ask. You can stop writing bullshit articles to get my attention. You got it. So, what are you going to do with it?"

"I—I didn't write it to—"

"Sweetheart, I respect you, don't ruin it by lying. You want me so I'm here."

"You are such a cocky bastard."

"Cocky yes, bastard no. I knew my daddy. He was a good man. Now enough talking. Let's go to dinner. I'm hungry. Let's do this."

"I don't date football players," Alex scoffed.

"Then consider it research, cause you need all the help you can get."

"What are you talking about? I did my research."

"That's even worse, if you got it wrong after research. You might want to reconsider your career path." He made a pained expression.

"What? What did I get wrong?" she challenged.

"Sweetheart, I'm not going to do your job for you. I don't see you running interference for me. Now get your coat. We have a date."

"I told you, I don't date football players."

"Why not? Not because you're not interested. Cause girl if you're trying to keep your thing for me on the down low, that ship has sailed. Everybody knows about it now. The first article people thought you had a bone to pick but now everyone knows you got it bad for me." He gave her a devilish grin.

Alex made an exasperated sound. "I don't have a bone to pick. I just write the facts." She was cute when she was annoyed. Pissing her off was more fun than he'd thought. He had just finished practice and had planned on going home and icing his shoulder but this was much more enjoyable.

God, she was cute like the younger sister of your friend you never noticed before then there she was. Nothing like the type he usually went for. Definitely not. Cane couldn't figure out what it was. Other than, Alex was a refreshing change. Nothing trophy wife about her, far too mouthy for that.

"You want facts, sweetheart. I'll give you a fact. You're looking at me like you want me to kiss you. At least, I think it's just a kiss you're after. Who knows. You're full of surprises."

"I don't want—"

"Sweetheart, what did I tell you about lying to me? Come on now. Respect the little intelligence you think I have." Cane closed the distance between them. He wrapped his arms around her and pulled her hard against his body. He spun them around so he could sit on the side of her desk so he wouldn't have to bend to kiss her. The corners of his mouth pulled upward into a smile. "I don't hear you saying no," he whispered.

Alex opened her mouth to protest but it was too late, Cane had already pulled her in. He used her open mouth as an opportunity for his tongue to explore. Her mouth was hot and tasted of cinnamon. God, she tasted good. And felt good. Her intoxicating scent almost had him losing his mind. He was kissing her to prove a point but he couldn't remember what it was.

Her body was so soft and yielding, molding into his own. Damn. He deepened the kiss, wanting more of her. Alex's hands went to his shoulders, holding onto him for support. She moaned into his mouth. The soft sound sending all non-essential blood coursing to his cock. She felt it, she must. It was pressed hard against her belly. Shit, he'd have her flat on her back in two minutes if they kept this up. This was not why he came here. Those days were behind him. His cock hadn't received the message yet. His body was ready to be ball deep inside her. His mind, however, was not on the same page. He wanted to mess around with her brain, not her body. This is what his brain kept on repeat. Yet his body ignored this idea.

With a groan Cane pulled away. Damn. Who was this woman? She looked like a librarian but she kissed like a…and the way he responded to her. Damn. He had not expected that. He cleared his throat. "Now that we cleared that up, you can stop pretending you didn't want to kiss me."

Alex's eyes narrowed. "Your tongue was in my mouth. I don't recall signing up for the oral inspection."

"Sweetheart, you moaned."

"Corn Fed, I make that sound with my vibrator too. Don't flatter yourself."

"You got to admit I'm better than a piece of vibrating silicone."

Alex threw back her head and laughed. "First of all, it was only a kiss and secondly, that's not saying much either. I'm better than my vibrator. I can make myself come in ninety seconds."

There was a flash of defiance in her eyes. He knew that look. He had exploited that look his entire childhood. He could make his younger brother; Cord play catch with a hornet's nest or jump off the train track bridge just by daring him. And the look in his brother's eyes was the same. Cord never said no to a dare. And neither did Alex. Cane would bet his pride on it.

"I'll do it in sixty," Cane said more casually than he felt. His cock strained against his trousers. He wanted her. Now.

Alex bit her bottom lip. He was instantly jealous of the white teeth sinking into the soft flesh. He wanted to be tasting those lips again. Alex took off her watch, and played with the buttons. "Sixty seconds, Corn Fed and then game over. No replays." The defiance in her eyes had morphed into desire. Her light brown irises glowed with it.

He was doing this. Tomorrow he would work on not having meaningless sexual encounters. Tonight, he was going to make her come. Cane made a show of lacing his fingers together and cracking them.

"Tell me when to start the clock." Alex tapped her phone as if she had not a care in the world.

"Oh, you'll know, sweetheart."

Cane lifted Alex up and set her down on top of her desk. Slowly he stripped her panties off and put them into his pocket. He pushed up her skirt until it was high on her thighs. He stood back and admired her pussy, black curls in a thin strip over full pink lips. Cane was overcome with the urge to bend down and lick those lips. His cock responded to the thought by thickening to almost painful proportion. Damn he wanted her. He really wasn't expecting this when he'd decided to stop by. He wanted to tease her a little, rile her up, then leave her panting and begging him to satisfy her. But now making her come was the only thing he could think about. He wanted to see her eyes hooded with desire. He wanted to push his finger inside her wet pussy as she moaned his name. Damn he was hard. He couldn't remember ever being this hard.

Cane pulled her knees apart. Her lips opened enough to showcase the glisten of her arousal on the intimate pink folds. She wanted this as much as he did. He could happily bury his head in there and not come up until morning. What did she taste like? God, he wanted to know. Needed to know.

Cane ran the back of his hand over her black curls. His index fingers separated her lips and found her clit. He stroked her softly. Usually he liked to go slow, learn a woman's body, make them both work for their release, but right now, he didn't have time or the resolve. He needed to make Alex come hard. And fast. Alex took in a sharp breath.

"Start the clock, sweetheart."

Her nostrils flared. Her response made it clear she hated when he called her sweetheart, so he would be sure to keep doing it.

Alex fumbled with the watch. It beeped when she hit start, counting down his minute. He got a minute in her pussy. Sixty seconds to touch, explore, enjoy. Damn she felt good. So soft and wet…hot. If his cock got any harder, he just might come in his pants.

Cane studied her face, watching for signs of arousal. Her eyes closed briefly, her lashes barely touching her cheek when his finger pressed into her. She liked it, being fucked with his finger. He smiled to himself, knowing he was pleasing her. His thumb rubbed tiny circles against her swollen clit. Alex's breath came in soft pants. She definitely liked it. Her eyes were closed now. They were squeezed tight as she concentrated on his hand fucking her.

Alex moaned. The sound deeper than the one she'd made in his mouth, more guttural, it reverberated through her. Over and over, he slid in and out of her until her hips bucked. "Ahh…" The beeper suddenly went off signaling their time was over.

"Should I take it into overtime?" Cane breathed against her ear.

Alex swallowed hard as she nodded.

"No, sweetheart. Tell me. Say the words. Tell me you want me to make you come."

"Yes…ahh….yes…please make me come."

Cane's smile deepened and a feeling of pride spread through his chest. His thumb rubbed harder against her swollen nub. He dropped his head and captured her mouth with his. Alex moaned into his mouth as she came. Her body shook as her inner walls tightened around his finger. Damn, he wished it was his cock deep inside her pussy. Next time. Next time it would be he promised himself. Cane waited until the last tremor faded from her body before he withdrew his slick digit.

Cane gently pulled down her skirt.

Alex opened her eyes and smiled. "Wow, Corn Fed. Football strings aren't the only thing you know how to grip."

Cane laughed. "Now that we've gotten that out of the way, can we go to dinner?"

Alex hopped off her desk and slid her skirt the rest of the way down. "I told you. I don't date football players. I mean it. I don't. Ever."

"But you're happy to let me get you off on your desk?"

Alex raised her hand. "You did good, Corn Fed. High five."

Cane laughed again. She wanted to high five after he made her come. No. He shook his head. That's not the game they were playing. He pulled her hard against him and kissed her, more deeply than before. He had to strain his neck to reach her, but it was worth it. He kissed her until she moaned. Satisfied, he pulled back.

"Get your coat, sweetheart. I made you come and now I'm buying you dinner. I usually do it the other way around. But we'll make this work. When we tell the grandkids this story, we will skip the part about you being finger fucked on the desk. We'll just leave it at you wrote a bullshit story and I bought you flowers because I'm a gentleman."

"Cane Clayburn, you are no gentleman," she objected as she reached for her coat. It was obvious she was going to entertain a dinner with him. Future family life was something else. That was the long game. Cane was amused and ready for the next play.

CHAPTER THREE

Alex had not planned for her path to ever cross with Cane Clayburn's again. She had written her article and was ready to move on to greener pastures. There were plenty of other football players to write about. Cane was a player. Not just on the field. He was known off the field for his conquests of socialites, models, influencers, you name it.

He'd had a reputation since college, probably even before that. Alex should have realized it years ago. But in a moment of weakness, she had been captivated by his deep blue eyes and large muscular frame. But it would never happen again. She hated that she hadn't been strong. She hated that she had succumbed to him in a way that felt familiar and also a betrayal to herself. After all these years, she thought she had grown. Like real growth. Personal growth.

Even the flowers he had sent were not enough to soften the anger she held for him. She only let them sit on her desk because they were too big to carry out of her office and the card just happened to be the right size for her bookmark. That was it.

The gall he had to show up on her turf in her office and make all sorts of claims about her. As if he had any idea about her feelings. What a ridiculous joke. It was so absurd.

Alex was not going to have any part of Cane and his suggestions. Not even the suggestion that she had a thing for him. Her eyes couldn't roll back in her head any farther. There would never be a day Alex had a thing for a football player. Especially not Cane Clayburn.

No way was she going to let that happen. Not in her office. Not anywhere. He deserved to be checked. But good grief, the man knew what he was doing. His large fingers were bigger than some erections she had experienced. It almost didn't seem fair that his fingers should be so huge. She could only imagine what lay underneath his pants.

The man was like a sculpted statue. He almost seemed unreal. Now she was sitting across from him at Perry's Steakhouse. His eyes were on the menu and Alex found herself unable to keep her own off of him. *Focus. Do not fall into the illusion that he is a nice guy. Well, he might be nice but nice doesn't cut it. Just enjoy the dinner, call a truce and move on.*

"Sweetheart, I know I'm hard to resist looking at but you'll need to be ready when the waiter comes." He winked at her.

"I'm always ready." She cut their eye contact and ran through the menu. She was famished. Once again, she had skipped lunch so she could run through a highlight reel one more time. There was something she had missed in her first article and she needed to figure out what it was. He mentioned again that her research was off. That she had missed something. What was it that he thought she had missed? Her insides were in a fury of confusion as to what she possibly could have overlooked. It made no sense. Research was her wheelhouse.

"That goes for two of us." He winked again. Alex rolled her eyes. *Seriously dude, a wink? What is this some 1970s sitcom?* Cane probably grew up without cable and is only able to relate to reruns of the Love Boat or some other tv show from that era.

"By the way, I need my panties back." Alex placed the

napkin in her lap. She really needed them back.

"No, sweetheart, those were my gift for playing so well." He raised his eyebrows. Underneath his dark brows were his deep blues. She cut their eye contact.

Alex scanned the room. It was filled with the typical Houston elite, even on a Monday night the place was packed. If Cane thought he deserved her panties, she would make him want something else even more. Time to play.

Alex scooted her chair closer to his. He glanced over at her and flashed his pearly white teeth. "Wanting to get to the cuddling part already?" he teased.

Alex smiled and lowered her hand under the table. She trailed her fingers up his massive thigh. It had to be bigger than both her legs combined. Further up she explored against the cotton material of his pants, until she reached the center. He was hard. Had he been hard this entire time or did he become instantly hard from the moment she touched him? Either way, this would be fun.

Cane cleared his throat and reached for the glass of water in front of him. This made Alex's heart flutter. She loved the idea that he was uncomfortable. Time to bring him down a notch.

She unzipped his pants and pulled out his erection. It was huge. Alex swallowed hard. She wanted to take a swig of her own water but that would be a distraction. She had him right where she wanted him. Gripped in between the palm of her hand. The white cloth on the table provided enough coverage for her to really work his cock over. Up and down, she stroked in fast repetitive motions. His eyes closed for a second. Cane's focus turned to Alex, like he wanted to say something or even do something. But they were in a crowded restaurant. All he could do was sit and enjoy the strokes or ask her to stop. But they both knew the latter wasn't going to happen.

The waiter appeared in front of them. Alex increased her speed. Would he come in front of the waiter or could he restrain himself? She continued to stroke as she eyed her menu.

"Oooh, I'll have the chicken breast, make sure it has lots of sauce. The creamy kind. I really like that creamy sauce." She licked her lips and gazed over at Cane's face. His eyes were on his menu. Like it was a rescue boat and his cock was the titanic about to go under. If they were alone Alex would have already gone under the table. The girth of his cock was so big she wanted to know what it would feel like in her mouth and down her throat. He was a challenge she wanted to take inside of her and run her tongue over the thick vein on the side. Damn he was big. She glided her finger over the tip of his cock. Liquid. She smiled. He was so close. She slowed down.

"And for you, sir?"

"Ah, yes. I'll get the prime rib, well done." He glanced at Alex. She bit her lip. Was he done? Not yet. He would be done when she was ready. She gripped him harder and picked up her pace.

"And the mashed potatoes, make sure you put extra butter on them. I like my potatoes wet." Cane's gaze returned to Alex.

The waiter's eyebrows furrowed.

"Also, can you sub my potatoes and give me the asparagus instead? Make sure they aren't cut. I like them to be really *long* stalks. And not over cooked. I like then hard. Long and hard." Alex slowed her pace into long tight strokes.

The waiter nodded and scribbled on his note pad.

"And extra butter on the side for me. I like to drizzle it over myself." Alex picked up her pace again and trailed her finger to the top of his cock. The liquid was back.

The waiter focused on his paper and left the table. Alex released her grip and stood up. "I'll be right back."

Cane grabbed her hand. "Really?"

"Really, sweetheart. Don't worry, I'll come back." Alex retracted her hand and made her way to the restroom.

CHAPTER FOUR

Cane took in a ragged breath. A scowl furrowed his brow. Alex had every intention of leaving him hard at the table knowing full well he could not get up with a massive erection. Little did she know, Cane never backed down from a challenge. He pushed his cock hard against his thigh and zipped his pants. Not the most comfortable, but worth it.

Cane pushed back from the table. He avoided eye contact with everyone as he crossed the crowded restaurant. Now was not the time to be stopped for an autograph. He caught up with Alex before she reached the restroom. He scooped her up in his arm and carried her into the accessible stall.

Her eyes widened in surprise, but in her hands was the foil packet of a condom. "I knew you wouldn't keep me waiting, Corn Fed."

He groaned internally. God she was hot. And prepared. Lucky for him, because he didn't have any condoms on him. In his house he had enough to stock a pharmacy. He always played safe. Always.

Cane sat her down and locked the door. This was not going to be his best performance. He was already ready to come. He was close before, but seeing Alex with the condom almost pushed him over the edge. There was nothing shy or coy about the woman's approach to sexuality. She fully embraced it, no apologies. Damn that was hot. It was so different from anyone he had ever even tried to conquer. He glanced down at her nipples, straining hard against the sheer material of her top. He needed to taste them. Cane pulled on the thin fabric. He couldn't reach her nipple because of her bra so he kissed her breasts as his fingers worked the peak through the layers of material.

"Shoot, I forgot my stopwatch," Alex said.

"I don't think we'd even have time to set it." Cane pulled her skirt up around her hips. He ran his hand over the curve of her ass.

"Ten-yard penalty if you can't make me come. Can you get it in the end zone, Corn Fed? Everyone is speculating about your performance on the field. But the real question is can you deliver the goods here." There was a challenge in her eyes.

He had to smile. Cane was cocky, he knew it, but Alex matched him on every level. "Sweetheart, you already know I can make you come." He tore open the packet and rolled the condom over his cock. He turned Alex around to face the mirror and reached between them and gently rubbed her tight opening. "Damn woman you are wet. Good, you'll be able to take all of me cause I ain't holding back."

"Bring it."

He wanted to tear the condom off and fuck her wet pussy with nothing in-between them. He wanted to feel her heat directly on his cock, no barriers. It was insane. He never had sex without protection. But a first date in a public bathroom was not the place to start. In an instant he thrust into her before he could do something crazy like pull off the condom and take her.

The mirror reflected her breasts bouncing through her blouse as he slammed harder into her. There was nothing more erotic than the visual of her eyes widen as he filled her.

She took in a sharp breath of air. He did not give her any time to adjust to his size; there was no holding back. Next time he would be slow. Next time. Hell yeah, there would be a next time. He didn't anticipate getting this woman out of his system for a good long time. How could he? This was not the woman he would put on his roster. She was not roster material.

Cane reached around and stroked her clit as he pounded into her, each thrust harder than the last, until he had lifted her up from the floor. "Oh yes," she cooed. Her head fell back against his chest. Her cheeks were red and her lips were swollen like he had kissed her. Fuck she was hot. How had he not noticed this before, in the locker room when she interviewed him? Was he fucking blind? The woman was sexy as hell. He couldn't hold back much longer. She was too tight...too hot. With a guttural growl Cane reached his climax He continued to stroke her until her pussy clenched around his cock as she came seconds after him.

His cock was exquisitely sensitive. Even through the condom he could feel each tremor. Next time no condom. He was going to feel her properly. Cane held her off the floor, waiting for her breathing to return to normal. He was never one to cuddle after sex but he wasn't ready to let her go, she felt too good in his arms, like her body was made for him.

Cane leaned down and kissed her hair. "I'm going to like having you as a girlfriend." He said it just to annoy her but the idea of it had its appeal. Sex on tap with a woman he found hot as hell. He got it now, why some of his friends and his older brother had forgone strange. There was something to knowing the sex was always going to be great. And with Alex, it was always going to be phenomenal. This wasn't a thought. It was fact.

Alex's head whipped round. "Do you need your ears checked too, Corn Fed? I thought it was just your shoulder that was letting you down. I don't date football players. Ever."

Cane smiled "Your argument would hold so much more water if my cock wasn't still hard inside you."

Suddenly Alex seemed aware of the situation. She squirmed trying to separate their bodies, but Cane held her off the ground impaled on him.

"You got skills. I will admit it. But I don't want a football player. I want someone good out of the bedroom, too. I want someone that can match my other skill sets and not let me down."

His mouth dropped open but he quickly rectified it. His cock was literally still hard in her pussy and she was insulting him. With a mumbled curse he pulled out of her. He yanked the condom off and wiped his dick clean. "Well, glad you enjoy my fucking." There was sassy and there was bitchy. Alex had moved into the second category. She thought he was stupid and used every opportunity to tell him. Not cool. Or true, but he had no intention of defending himself to her.

Cane didn't wait to make sure Alex was ready for him to open the door. He tossed the condom in the trash and went back to the table. Their food had already arrived. He sat down and tore into the prime rib. At least the meal would be a satisfying experience.

A few minutes later Alex returned. "Ooh nice. They remembered the extra sauce. I do really like it." She smiled up at him as if nothing had happened. She chewed her chicken and let out a contented sigh. "So good," she said after she swallowed. "I haven't been here in ages." Her eyes glanced to the side like she was thinking. "Oh, that's right. I was here with the cardiologist from Texas Children's hospital. He was vegan. Why would a vegan bring his date to a steakhouse? Yeah, that was never going to end well."

Unbelievable. Alex was telling him about another date. If she told him about the sex he was going to need to get up and punch a wall. Why did he care? He didn't. She liked smart professional guys. He liked tall blonds. Everyone had a type. And he wasn't hers, apparently.

"Creamed spinach. Oh, my favorite." Alex took a forkful off his plate without asking. "Mmm…you can taste the nutmeg. So good. Taste it, Corn Fed. I know you're probably not a fan of green things, but oh my god, this is a party in my mouth."

Cane smiled despite his mood. She enjoyed her food with the same passion she enjoyed her sex. Against all normal roster choices, she was hot. Damn it. Why did she have to be hot and such a bitch? She wasn't hot when he'd first met her, just a bitch. He liked that way better. He didn't want to have sex with that Alex. That Alex was wholesome and slightly frumpy.

"Taste the spinach with the mashed potatoes. Those two need to get married and have little vegetable babies. Or skip the marriage and just have delicious culinary bastards. Either way you need to try it." Alex held the fork to his lips. He paused for a second before he took the bite. "Right? So good." Alex smiled.

"Yeah, it's good," he admitted.

"Admit it, Corn Fed. I just took your green vegetable cherry, didn't I? And it was good."

Cane shook his head and smiled. "Nope not my first. My sister-in-law Cheyenne is vegan. I only eat green things when she cooks."

The space between Alex's eyes furrowed. "A vegan called Cheyenne? Sounds like she is trying to be Cheyenne Ford."

"Not trying, she *is* Cheyenne Ford. Or she was until she married my brother Colt. She is Cheyenne Clayburn now."

"Shut the front door. Your brother is married to Country's Darling? She has sold like a billion records just this year."

"Yep, that's Cheyenne. Try listening to the album knowing every song is written about your brother. God only knows what they get up to with spurs. Have you heard that song?"

"Heard it? I love it! It is my shower jam."

27

"I'd love to hear that." Cane laughed.

Alex shook her head. "No, Corn Fed. I don't sing for anybody. Trust me, you would thank me for sparing you from that. How did I not know Cheyenne Ford was your sister-in-law?"

"Because you do a piss poor job at research." Cane smeared horseradish on his prime rib.

The color returned to Alex's cheeks. He had found her Achilles Heel. She hated to have her work questioned. Duly noted.

"You keep saying that. What did I get wrong in the article?"

He shook his head. "Nope. You lost the right to have me fact check two bullshit articles ago."

"Everything I said was factually correct. I spent all day watching your highlights. I got it right."

"All day, huh? I knew you were into me. Sweetheart, you should have just asked me out. I might have said yes. No guarantees but it would have been a hell of a lot easier than all of this."

"Hmm." Alex took another bite of spinach from his plate.

"Now if this were a date, I would happily answer any of your questions. Cause that's just manners."

"Good idea. I will ask one of your ex-girlfriends. Thank you." Alex finished off his spinach. When the waiter came back Cane was going to order her more so he could hear her make the little contented sigh after every bite.

"My last steady girlfriend was when I was fourteen, lasted six glorious weeks. She let me touch her boobs. Ah, Lilly. I wonder what she is doing these days."

Alex shook her head. "Shut it, Clayburn. You have more exes than there are constellations in this galaxy. So, stop pretending to be virtuous."

"Sweetheart, I wouldn't even know how to pretend to be virtuous. Were you not the one I was screwing in the bathroom ten minutes ago? No virtue here, guaranteed.

Yeah, I screw a lot of women but none of them were girlfriends. None of them can tell you anything you wouldn't find in your highlights reel." He took a sip of water. "No actually wait, some can tell you that I make the best eggs benedict this side of the Mason Dixon. Spend the night tonight, I'll show you."

Alex scoffed. "Ha! Are you serious? No long-term girlfriends. Arg, I wish I had that factoid for the article. Next one."

"You can't write another article about me. It's getting a bit desperate. Everyone knows you want me. Have some self-respect," he teased.

"Self-respect. Ha! Says the man who has a sex life that would make Caligula blush."

"Had. I'm a new man. Turned over a new leaf, sweetheart. Only sleeping with my girlfriend until further notice." He winked at her over his glass. The comment got just the reaction he'd hoped for; her cheeks went a darker shade of red.

"Because I have self-respect, I would *never* be your girlfriend."

"Doth protest too much. Should we edit this part out of the story too, when we tell the grandkids? Lord, we are going to have to do a heavy edit on our official story. No making you come on your desk before the date. No sex in the bathroom during the first date—"

"This is not a date," she interrupted.

"Really? What is it? We had sex and I took you to dinner. This is a date. Not the best I've been on. But not the worst." He smiled.

"This is me eating because I'm hungry. The sex was me screwing because I was horny. It is really quite simple. Should I write it down so you can reference it or maybe include illustrations because you're not much of a reader?"

"Illustrations please. Those are some pictures I would like to see. Though to be fair, the image of you coming while I fucked you against the sink, is burned in here." Cane tapped his head. "Thank you for that. I will be using that to get off for the foreseeable future. Good stuff. Shower time just got fun again."

Alex laughed. "You're ridiculous. You know that, right?"

"And that is your type, apparently. Bet you didn't know that. Feel free to think about me when you get off. We both know you will."

"So cocky." Alex shook her head and laughed.

"And yet you did not deny it."

Alex gave him a hard stare. "You want to know if I will think about you next time I masturbate? Yeah, probably. There is a ninety percent chance I will unless I hear Luke Bryan on the radio first, then it will be him, but otherwise it's all you, Corn Fed. But here is the thing. Yeah, you can get me off. But would I ever take you home to meet my dad? Or call you to have a deep and meaningful conversation? Or trust you not to screw around the moment you catch the scent of another women? No. The answer to all those questions is no, in case you're not connecting the dots. You are not boyfriend material. You are give-me-great-orgasms-that-I-can-think-about-later material."

"Because I'm a football player?" he asked indignantly. "You know that is just my job, that's not actually who I am."

"I know who you are. You are a player, on and off the field."

"Wow, you really hate football players."

Alex shook her head. "I don't hate anybody. Well, other than my next-door neighbor because he plays Christian Rock while he has sex and I should not have to listen to that through the wall. That is some crazy shiz. But no, Corn Fed, I don't hate you. As for football. I love it, hence my job. I'm not crazy about the players, but I love the game."

Cane stopped to consider her words. He ran a hand through his hair. For once he had no idea what to say. She was effectively shutting him down. She wanted nothing to do with him. Okay. Well, that was his pride taking a direct hit. What was he doing here? He shook his head. No wait, it didn't make sense. "What about that picture on your desk? You are surrounded by the OU team and you look pretty happy about it."

Her face changed, slightly taken aback. "You saw that? That's my dad. He is the head coach at OU. That's why I'm smiling in the picture. I am hanging out with my dad."

"Your dad is the head coach at OU? So, did one of the players break your heart when you were in college? Is that where this no player policy came from?"

"Nope. I didn't go to Oklahoma. And my dad would have benched any player who looked at me."

"What? You didn't go to OU? I thought that is where the article came from. A rival school thing."

Alex's eyes narrowed in confusion. "I went to UT. Same as you, Corn Fed. We were there at the same time."

It was Cane's turn to be confused. "You went to UT?"

"Yep." She rolled her eyes and sighed. "I bleed orange."

No, she was kidding. He would remember her. Surely a woman like Alex would have made some sort of impression if they'd crossed paths. He dismissed the thought; it was a big school.

"So, what kind of guys do you bring home to meet your dad?"

She let out a stream of air. "I'll let you know when I bring one home."

"What? After giving me a hard time about being a man-whore, you have never had a serious relationship? Hello pot, I'm the big dicked kettle."

Alex smiled. "You're very proud of that big dick, aren't you?"

"I am, now continue telling me what a hypocrite you are."

"I'm not a hypocrite. I've had plenty of boyfriends just none that I brought home to meet my dad."

"Why?" he asked. "Are you not close? Is that it?"

Alex thought about it for a minute. "No. My dad and I are very close…in our own way. He raised me alone and he did a fairly great job, right?" She tried to smile but it did not reach her eyes. "No, we are close, as close as we can be. My dad isn't really a demonstrative person. I know he loves me. I hope he is proud of me. But he doesn't tell me either of those things." Alex shrugged her shoulders, clearly uncomfortable with the direction the conversation had taken. "I mean, we talk most days. It's just us. I don't have any siblings. So, we are close."

"What do you talk about?" Cane wasn't going to let it go. *Not demonstrative*, from the woman who high fives after sex. The man must be cold.

"What?"

"What do you talk about?" he repeated.

"You know normal stuff. Sports, hunting, sometimes politics. Usual stuff."

"Ah, I see. Normal guy stuff."

"Yeah… no…wait. Normal stuff. Period."

"Don't have to explain it to me, sweetheart. I get it."

Alex stared at him like she was debating asking him what he meant. Finally, her curiosity got the best of her and she did. Cane liked that about her. He could bend her to his will by daring her or appealing to her curiosity. He would definitely be using those things to his advantage. "What is it you think you know?"

"You're the son he always wanted. You're a sports reporter. You go hunting with him. Even your name."

Alex gave him a dubious look. "No, I think my dad would have been worse with a son, actually. He just shut down after my mom died. He was so in love with her. He still is. He can't even talk about her. It's too much emotion for him so he shuts those conversations down."

"What was she like? Your mom?"

"Um…nothing like me, apparently. She was blond, big blue eyes. She was a cheerleader, Dallas Cowboys. That's how they met, when my dad was playing. Why are you smiling? Please don't tell me you think my mom sounds hot."

Cane wasn't even aware he was smiling. He just felt like smiling around her. Despite her, actually. She was caustic but strangely engaging. "Nope not thinking about your mom being hot, I was thinking that two of our kids would probably be blond and blue eyed like me and the others would have dark hair like you. Same in my family, two blonds and two have black hair."

The comment was designed to rile her which it did. Her face contorted in disgust.

"Dear lord, that sounds like a fate worse than death. Four children. No, just no."

He wasn't expecting such a strong reaction to the mention of children. "You don't want kids?"

"Oh god, no. And kids don't want me. I can't even keep houseplants alive. You're looking at me like I sprouted another head. You want kids, don't you?"

Cane nodded. "Yep, four."

"Well good luck finding someone to breed with. Make sure she is big. Birthing your babies is not going to be easy. God, I feel sorry for that poor woman already." Alex shuddered.

"I will remind you of that when you're in labor with Katrina. We're naming our daughter after my mom. Hope that is okay. The second one can be named after your mom. What was her name?" Alex's cheeks were now the same shade as the wine at the next table. Teasing her would never get old. Between that and sex, Cane would always be entertained with her.

"Her name was Sandra and I would never name a child after her." Alex's eyes went dark. She glanced at the door like she wanted to run away. "Wow, I should have ordered wine. This conversation just got a bit too deep. My mom killed herself when I was six weeks old. She had postpartum depression. So, I definitely would not be naming a child after her."

"I'm sorry. Is that why you don't want to have children?"

Alex took a deep breath. "What are you doing to me,

Corn Fed? I never talk about my mom."

Cane shrugged. "It's my skill. I can get anybody to spill their secrets. And I can make you come in less than sixty seconds. So, there is that, too."

Alex laughed. "No, the timer went off. You were in overtime with that one."

"True. I'll do better next time."

"Ha! There won't be a next time. Nice try, though."

"Oh, there will be a next time. And a next. Though sometimes I will make you wait for it. Beg actually. That can be fun, too. Dessert?"

"You are so cocky. You know that, right, and yes on dessert. Always yes on dessert. The cheesecake here is amazing."

"Did you order it when you were here with the vegan?" He couldn't resist asking, why he cared was beyond him.

"Hmm…was it with him? Um…no. Now I remember. It was with the pilot."

"You date a lot," Cane said, surprised by his jealousy. Cane wasn't jealous. Cane was Mr. Laidback. Never staked his claim, never jealous.

"You screw a lot. Are we stating random facts? Ooh, my turn again. You have massive hands. Like obscenely big. Ooh, ooh. I got another: Far too many of your passes go to running backs. You're very predictable, Corn Fed. Oh, and you struggle on the drop back. Want me to keep going?"

"No, you're okay."

She wagged her finger. "See. I told you I do my research. I know all about you."

The waiter came over. "How was everything?"

"Great, thank you," Alex replied with a smile.

"Would you like to order coffee or dessert?"

"I'll have the peanut butter cheesecake. Thank you."

The waiter turned to Cane. "And for you, sir?"

"No thanks, I'm good."

Alex shook her head. "Don't say that and then try to share with me. The last guy who tried that got a fork in his hand. I don't want Texan fans blaming me when you fumble. You got that covered on your own." She smiled demurely, pretending to be sweet when they both knew she was anything but.

God, he wanted to kiss her and then take her back in the bathroom for another round. And then talk to her. He wanted to talk to a woman, not just screw her. He had heard of this phenomenon, though he had never experienced it firsthand.

Cane grabbed her phone off the table.

"What are you doing?"

"I'm giving you my number."

"I didn't ask for your number."

"Consider it a gift."

Alex shook her head. "Does this cocky thing work for you usually?"

"I do okay."

"I bet you do, Corn Fed."

The waiter returned with Alex's cheesecake. Alex sighed when she took the first bite. She took a forkful and held it up to his lips. "You really need to try this. It's right up there with orgasms on my list of favorite things. Oh, and coffee. I can't forget coffee."

"Nice," Cane agreed after he swallowed. "Which is your favorite? You can only have one of those things for the rest of your life."

"Ooh, that is hard." Alex took another bite of cheesecake as she thought. "My first thought would be coffee. I mean, I need that every morning to start the day. But once I went cold turkey, I would be fine after a week or two. But I would be jonesing for cheesecake and orgasms forever."

"So, which would you pick?"

Alex shook her head. "Nope. I can't choose. That is like me asking which of your six children is your favorite?"

"Four. We're having four children," he reminded her.

"Oh god, no. Stop saying that. You will put me off my

cheesecake."

"God forbid. We can discuss our family after dessert."

"I would rather discuss your inability to identify a blitz. I'm full. Here, you have the last bite. This cheesecake is too good not to eat."

Cane finished her dessert as Alex sat back in her seat.

"Come home with me." Cane wanted to make love to her properly and talk. He actually wanted to speak to her, know her opinion on things. And he wanted to make her breakfast, see her in his jersey with nothing else on.

Alex sighed as she opened her purse and pulled out a wad of cash and laid it on the table.

"What are you doing? I'm paying for dinner," Cane said.

"No, you're not. This isn't a date. I really don't date football players, Corn Fed. No exceptions. Thanks for the sex. Your game is even better off the pitch. See you on the field."

Alex left without looking back.

As she walked away, Cane felt deflated, like someone had taken away something he didn't know he wanted.

Damn. What was that? He could only shake his head. He ignored the cash on the table and paid with his card. As Cane signed his name on the receipt he noticed a silver packet underneath the green bills. That couldn't have been a mistake. Cane put the condom in his pocket and ran his hand through his hair. Obviously, this was an invitation. Being able to read a play on the field was what made him one of the best quarterbacks in the league. This was junior varsity level material but he was game.

CHAPTER FIVE

In thirty minutes, Alex was going to have her third date with Dean Fairley. On paper he was perfect. Thirty-two, tall, handsome, he was a man with conviction. Three years ago, he'd opened his own chiropractic business. Alex had been a former client. Dean knew what to do with his hands in the office but she had yet to experience them on a more personal level.

Alex examined herself via her phone. Cane Clayburn. Seriously, the man had amazing skills but the mark on her breast was not okay. She snapped a photo. This would not go on Instagram but it would be texted to him. Before she could second guess herself, she hit the send button. No message, he would know it was her. Then again, maybe this is his thing. Maybe he has left his mark on lots of women and he wouldn't know whose boob it was. It wasn't her entire boob, just the image of the hickey. Seriously, who does that? Alex hadn't received a hickey since high school. Well, no, there was that one in college. How apropos. She shook her head. He had no idea.

"Nice. But next time angle the camera lower if you want to send me a pic of your tits."

Alex rolled her eyes. This man was so utterly ridiculous.

"That won't ever happen." She hit send again, too soon.

"Sweetheart, it already did. I've got your tit as the contact pic for your number."

Alex groaned. *"Well, this will be the last time I contact you."*

"What did I tell you about lying?" His text speed was a bit surprising given the amount of time he probably had to form a sentence in his head and then figure out how to spell the words.

"I won't be contacting you. No need for a story and the mark on my chest is definitely not approved. You've been benched permanently."

Alex threw her phone in her purse. She had to hurry. Now, even if Dean had wanted to make it to second base it wasn't going to happen. Alex was not going to be seen with a hickey on her chest. That would obviously give the wrong impression. Dean had boyfriend potential written all over him.

Despite this, she was not ready to be alone in a car with him. Alex needed to have an out. A way to leave for any reason. She didn't want to be stranded. Alex prepared for every moment in her life. The lack of real parental assistance caused her to grow up early. Despite her dad being a constant figure, he was not there for emotive moments, or thoughts or assistance that a girl would need. He was more like "here's some cash—be safe." As if she would have known at the age of eight what that meant.

Prior to the date, there were a few texts, nothing of significance but enough to get to an agreed upon place to meet at Masraff's. Alex was famished. She had perused the menu enough times to know this was a place she could eat. She always had a big appetite. College seemed to really take her under with her intake to calorie outtake. But since then, she knew to counter act her appetite she would need to expend major energy. Not that she enjoyed it. But she did enjoy the food. She was not going to give that up. If her body size stepped above a curvy six, she would find herself in the job line in search of something with less expectations for her body size. Alex knew this and fought it. Every day.

Masraff's was a place she had been on a few prior dates. She knew the menu but still scanned through it before the date as if in preparation for a big exam. The jumbo crab cake had been on her mind all day. The photo of the pink plump flesh with that drizzle of butter. Her stomach growled as if it agreed with her thoughts.

She put on her crème jacket over her pumpkin a-framed dress. This was not the outfit Alex had intended for tonight's date but given the location of the hickey she had to wear something with a higher neckline. Her phone buzzed from her purse as she turned off the ignition to her car.

"You can't bench your boyfriend. And the mark...Consider yourself branded."

Alex rolled her eyes. He was too much. Branded. If she wasn't so weak from hunger, she would cancel the date with Dean and find Cane and brand him. With something hot. Her chest tightened and her cheeks warmed. No. She was not going to be excited about him. Not anymore. She would save her alone time for someone else's image. Definitely, not Cane Clayburn.

She marched into Masraffs and let the hostess lead her through the crowded restaurant to Dean's table. Alex leaned in and kissed his cheek.

"I hope you weren't waiting long?"

Dean glanced at his watch. "Let's see I got here at seven-fifteen, our scheduled time, and it is now seven-twenty-eight so I have been waiting for approximately fifteen minutes give or take a couple." He laughed.

Alex let out a laugh, too. Good grief. His sense of humor drained her soul. No matter how much she had wanted this to work, it would be their last date. There was no way Alex could stomach anymore of Dean. Thank goodness they were at a five-star restaurant. She reminded herself to take pleasure in the meal and the atmosphere. Out of the corner of her eye a large man waved at her. No. She sucked in a sharp breath.

"Are you alright?" Dean grabbed her hand.

Alex jerked it back. "Oh, sorry. Yes, I'm fine. I just—"

"Oh look, its Cane Clayburn. Wow, imagine that, the two of us here at the same restaurant as him. Wow. This is so cool. I wonder if he would let us take a photo with him?"

Internally, Alex grimaced. There was absofuckingloutely no way she would ever take a photo with Cane. No. She focused her eyes on the menu. Food. *Find your happy place. This restaurant is filled with choices of happiness. Delicious calorie laden treats that will be like an orgasm in your mouth. Yes. Yum.*

"Oh, wow. He's walking this way. I think he's coming to our table. Crap. Uh…how does my hair look?" Dean tapped Alex's shoulder. She didn't need a wakeup call. She needed an exit plan. Why was this happening to her? Alex was already on a boring date but now she was about to be confronted by Cane on the boring date. She squeezed her eyes tight. Maybe he wouldn't see her.

"Alex, is it okay?" Dean nudged her arm again.

She glanced at him. "Yes, it looks great."

Cane was five feet from the table. She dropped her head under the table in search of something…anything.

"Alex, what are you doing?" Dean lifted up the cloth and peered at her.

"Oh…I…um…dropped my watch. I can't seem to find it."

"The one on your wrist?" Dean raised an eyebrow at her.

"No, I have a spare one. It was in my lap and then it slipped." Alex moved her hands around the floor. If she had dropped a watch, it would not be hard to see. The floor was impeccably clean.

"Found you." Cane's deep blue eyes sparkled when they locked with hers. No. Why? Why couldn't he keep going?

Alex let out a slight laugh. "Ha. Yes. I found it." She pretended to grab something off the floor and stuff it into her purse. Cane was like a giant as he gazed at her from his full height. She immediately wanted to stand up so she wouldn't be so incredibly small in her seat.

"Cane Clayburn, I'm a big fan. Like huge. Like I've got every single one of your jerseys and even the one from the build a bear workshop." Dean laughed. "I probably shouldn't admit that. But seriously, man, huge fan."

Cane nodded his head. "Thanks, it's always nice to have fans." He eyed Alex. Her jaw was clenched tight. *Move on. Go back to your table or leave the restaurant.*

"Hey, would you be willing,..um…would it be okay if I got your picture?" Dean reached into his pocket and pulled out his phone.

"Sure thing, man. Happy to give you a picture. Pictures are fun. My girlfriend sent me one today that man…anyway, let's take the photo." Cane's gaze burned on her skin causing little pinpricks of desire and mortification. Not a pleasant combination. Why did he have to be such an ass? And so damn hot.

Dean stood up. "Here Alex, take a few just in case I blink, okay?"

Alex used every morsel of self-control not to run from the table and this horribly awkward moment. The way Cane's eyes flickered dark blue with sparks of turquoise made her want to hit him on the head and shake off that look. It was obvious he was enjoying this moment. She pressed her lips together and stood up.

"Sure." She took the phone from Dean and hit the circle button enough times that she had hoped one of them would have ejected Cane from the restaurant, but much to her dismay it didn't.

"So, is this a date?" Cane focused on Alex's face.

Alex bit her lip.

"Our third." She smiled at him and squeezed Dean's hand.

Cane glanced down for a second. It was what he did during a blitz play. Alex had studied Cane's reactions on reels too many times to count. He was caught off guard. Good.

"Enjoy your meal. I hope you don't lose anything else

under the table." Cane's body moved passed the table. Alex wanted to respond but there was nothing left to say. She appeared like the player she had called him and she wasn't. She did date but not sleep around. She had only had sex with Cane because he'd challenged her and he was incredibly hot, sexy and God, so big. And other things that only she seemed to be aware of. Why did he have to be such an ass? And why did she have to be stuck on this date with such a boring guy. Order the meal and get out. That was her game plan.

CHAPTER SIX

"Was that Alex Martin over there?" one of Cane's teammates asked. They were there to unwind after practice, get a nice meal in before the pressure of the season. Seeing Alex on a date with another man was definitely not helping Cane unwind. It was doing the opposite of that. He was ready to punch someone. Hard. In the throat. Seriously, that was her type? That dude was scrawny, barely six feet tall and two hundred pounds. Tiny men must be her thing. Cane ground his teeth together until his jaw ached. What was the tit picture about? Fuck! Did she send it from her date with another guy? Not cool.

"Earth to Clayburn."

Cane's head shot up. "Sorry, what were you saying?"

"Alex Martin. She's hot in that girl-next-door kind of way. I would totally do her." Dave Poston laughed. The other guys snorted their approval.

"What about you? Would you do her?" Dave asked, as he socked Cane in the arm.

I already have. Cane remained silent. His temples throbbed. He just wanted to go home and drag Alex with him.

"Dude, I bet she is dirty. Like filthy. The plain ones

43

always are."

Plain? Who the fuck was Dave looking at? There was nothing plain about Alex. The woman was hot. And she was on a date with another guy. Shit his head hurt. Punching someone would help that. At least he thought so.

"What do you think? I bet she would take it in the ass." Dave laughed.

Cane's head snapped around. If Dave said one more thing about Alex, he was going to be the one getting punched. And that would do fuck nothing for team morale, having the quarterback put a beat down on the tight end. But Cane would if Dave spoke another word about her. Time to shut this conversation down. "Dude, we all know it's you that wants something in your ass. I don't think she has the parts to service you, buddy."

The rest of the guys laughed, successfully diffusing the situation and Cane's need for blood. At least temporarily.

The waitress seated the team near the window. Several tables had been pushed together. Cane picked a seat where he could watch Alex. Immediately he regretted it. His eyes were on the table as he watched Alex take a forkful off the dude's plate. What the fuck? Cane was fine with Alex taking bites from his plate but not this douche's. Her mouth, nor her fork, or any other part of her should be near this other guy.

What was that about? She swallowed the bite and then smiled. Shit. Now she was laughing. The douche was funny. He made her laugh. Yep, Cane was going to punch someone tonight.

Alex reached over the table and wiped something off the guy's face with her thumb. And then she licked it. Fuck no. Not happening. Cane pushed back from the table. He wasn't hungry. He could eat nine thousand calories on a good day, but not today.

Shit, where were her hands? If she was giving this guy a hand job, Cane would murder him. Straight up, rip his arms off and beat him to death with them. What the fuck did she see in that guy? He used more product than she did.

Cane stopped himself before he got to Alex's table. Fuck. What was he doing? She wasn't really his girlfriend. He just said that to rile her. He had no claim on her.

And he didn't want one. Not his type. He liked blonds. That's right, not his type. He needed a drink. Maybe after a beer Alex would stop being his type. Cane didn't drink during the season. But tonight was an exception.

"Lovestreet, please," Cane motioned at the bartender. "Cane Clayburn!" a woman squealed from behind him.

He turned to see Miss Texas waving frantically. She was coming toward him. Shit! What was her name? They met once at a bar opening. What was her name? Tiffany? Brittney? Shit. He knew it once. She was coming closer. Her movements were slightly hindered by her tight bandage dress and the Lucite stilettoes. She looked like she had just left work mid-pole dance.

"Hey, you." Cane stood up and wrapped an arm around her waist and leaned down to kiss her cheek. Smooth. All women like being called *you*. She smelled of roses. Suddenly he remembered. Monica and they met at a boat party and had had sex in her car. The smell of roses brought it all back. She'd just laid there like she was trying not to mess up her hair even though she had enough hair spray in it to survive a wind tunnel.

"Haven't seen you around in forever. Where have you been hiding?"

Cane forced a smile. He glanced behind him to see what Alex was doing but she had already left. Annoyance simmered in him. Did she go home with that guy? Cane gave his head a terse shake. *Stay in the moment, man.* "Yeah. I've been around. Just working. Um…how have you been? How's…things?" He didn't know what else to say. He had had sex with her but damn if he remembered having a conversation with her. Did she have a job outside of being a beauty queen? Was that her job? Surely, she had to have a job. Wearing a crown and a sash couldn't pay the bills, could it?

"Good. Good. Everything is good. So busy. You know with all the appearances and charity work."

Charity work. What kind of charity work did she do? Was there a charity giving out tiaras to underprivileged kids he didn't know about, because clearly America needed that. Cane nodded because he didn't have anything to say to her. They had absolutely nothing in common except sex and she had phoned that in.

"So…" she said, pouting.

She was waiting for him to say something. But what? What did she want from him?

Monica reached out and stroked the flat plain of his stomach and smiled coyly. Really? That is what she was after. She wanted sex. He hadn't got her off; she barely participated. What was the point? He made a point of only fucking women who were up for it.

"So," he said, not playing along. He wasn't interested.

Her pout turned into a frown.

"Cane, are you going to make me ask?"

His brow arched in question.

"I will. If I have to." She batted her lashes at him. The desired effect was seduction but her false lashes reminded him of a moth desperately beating its wings to take off.

Cane sighed. He didn't have any other plans. He had planned on stopping by Alex's after the team dinner. But that wasn't happening now. Cane gave Monica a hard stare. She was pretty enough. God only knew what she looked like under the mask of makeup but with all the war paint she had "trophy" written all over her. Cane took in a deep breath. There were worse ways to spend a Tuesday night. He wasn't into her but maybe it would make him less into Alex.

Monica squeezed his bicep. Okay, let's do this. "Can I get you a drink?"

Monica's smile broadened exposing perfect veneers. "I thought you would never ask."

Cane wrapped his fingers around the neck of the bottle and told himself not to think about what Alex was doing, or with who. Monica sipped her cosmopolitan and talked at him. He wasn't listening but she didn't seem to notice or care. The drink was just to make the sex they were going to have seem less tawdry. It was a date, if they had drinks, not just fucking a random stranger because you couldn't be fucking the one you really wanted to be with.

Monica pushed back from the bar. "My place?"

Perfect. He could leave as soon as he was done. Cane followed her to her car. Her hips swayed when she walked. It could be considered sexy but he just wasn't feeling it. Fuck, what was he doing? He was about to go home with Miss Texas and he could not even manage a bit of excitement. He was going to be the one phoning it in tonight. Cane sighed. Maybe once they got started, he would be into it. Only one way to find out. Cane pulled Monica's hand and spun her around. He pulled her close and pressed his lips to hers. Her mouth opened for him without any coaxing. She was up for it today. Maybe last time she was having an off day. Her tongue darted into his mouth, wet, aggressive and in command. He liked that. Usually.

Nothing. He felt nothing. There was no spark, no desire to take it to the next level or even keep going. Nothing. Shit.

Cane pulled back. He ran a hand through his hair. "It's um…it's late." The excuse sounded lame even to him. It wasn't even 8 p.m. "I have practice in the morning." Cane rubbed his eyes searching for excuses.

"Yeah. That's cool. Its late," Monica agreed. She unlocked her car and got in without turning around or saying goodbye.

Cane shook his head as she drove away. Miss Texas. He could be ball deep in Miss Texas tonight but he was going to be in a piss poor mood thinking about Alex and some other guy. Cane was an idiot, no two ways about it.

Damn it, Alex had gotten under his skin. Cane didn't want Miss Texas or any other woman. He wanted Alex. And he was going to have her.

CHAPTER SEVEN

The shower had not provided the experience Alex had hoped for but neither had this day. She was ready to call it a night. After what should have been a delicious meal, she drove herself home and tried to release some of the frustration that Cane had given her but for the first time in a long time Alex was unable to bring herself to orgasm which made her even more pissed at him. She put on her Salvatore t-shirt. Maybe one of the Salvatore brothers could give her the inspiration she needed to bring herself to orgasm. Alex made her way down the hall. The doorbell sounded.

"What in the world?" Alex paced back to the living room and peered out the peep hole of her door. Through the small hole stood a large man. With a face she had wanted to forget. Not show up on her doorstep.

Seriously? Why? Why was he here? She would tell him to bounce and sniff around someone else's doorstep. She was not interested in leftovers unless they were from a Michelin rated restaurant. Then maybe. Cane was not going to play her again. She would not be the golden retriever ever again. She would be the black cat. No, better yet, she wouldn't tell him to bounce. It was fine. He could come in and make her come and then move on. For good. No more replays, this was not some sort of ESPN highlight reel of her life. This was a mashup of good feelings in the moment and a bad aftertaste that had always left her in need of a full body detox. That began with her mind.

She opened the door. His massive body didn't even seem like he could make it through her doorway.

"I knew you would be alone." He nodded. God, he was so full of himself. It was almost as if he was going to high five his own hand. Yes, she was alone. She lived alone. This was her place. Who else would be here?

"How did you find out where I live?" She inspected his face. The sides of his mouth pulled up and he flashed her his damn pearly whites. Her own mouth tried to pull up in response but she forced a straight line of her lips. She would not be persuaded by his charm.

"Some of us do better research than others." He moved past her as if he too lived there. Arg. Alex groaned.

"Sweetheart, I haven't even touched you yet and you're moaning. Sometimes I even impress myself." He made his way into her kitchen and put a bag in her freezer.

"Sometimes? You always seem impressed with yourself. And that was a groan not a moan. You might want to add sounds to things you should work on."

Cane laughed. "Yea, I'll add that to my list. But I don't seem to have any problems making you moan." His eyes ran along her body. He had seen her before but his gaze was different like he'd just noticed her. Alex swallowed. She was not in a state to take in gazes like that. Especially not from him. She pressed her fingertips into her palms to center herself. Gain back control of her emotions.

Alex tugged on her shirt. She should change. No. He should just leave. She was going to bed. A small part of her didn't want to ask him to leave. And another part of her really wanted him to stay. And an even bigger part wanted to take him to bed. Not to sleep. Absolutely no sleep.

"Salvatore? Who does he play for?" Cane pulled on the

fabric of her jersey. Her cheeks were on fire. This was not the shirt to have on in front of Cane.

"Mystic Falls." She let out a slight giggle. It didn't matter. Cane wouldn't know anything about The Vampire Diaries and his brain capacity wasn't large enough to remember this conversation. Besides, they wouldn't see each other again so it was fine.

"So, do you sleep commando?"

"Commando? I'm not a man." She rolled her eyes.

"Sweetheart, I know you're not a man. If you were, I wouldn't be here." He tugged on her shirt again.

"Cane are you unable to form the words that you are thinking, is that it? Did you really just want to know if I had on anything under my shirt?"

He laughed. "Sweetheart, if I wanted to know if anything was under your shirt, I would just take it off."

Her cheeks warmed but it was nothing like the temperature between her thighs. God, he made her so hot. She wished it weren't true but he was irresistible. He was fucking irresistible. She had absolutely no self-control around him. With her mind, her words, and definitely not her actions.

"Yea, maybe you should just take off your own clothes so I can inspect your body and make sure you didn't suffer any injuries since our locker room interview."

He grinned. "Now you're talking, sweetheart. You want a show, is that what you want?"

"Yea, give me a show. Here let me put some music on for you."

Alex didn't even have to scan through her music. She knew the exact song Cane should strip to. Her blood quickened as she pulled up her Spotify Sexy Playlist.

"Let me hear you say Hey Ms. Carter." Beyonce called out from her speakers. Alex had surround sound. It was imperative for when she watched the game. She wanted to feel like she was actually on the field.

Cane glanced down for a second and then flashed his

wicked grin. It was obvious he wanted to dance for her. He was proud of his body. The man had a zillion photos of his muscles on all of his social feeds. His most recent profile pic was a close up of his huge muscular arms. From his forearms to his bicep and finally his large squared shoulders. He was perfection. His body. His body was perfection. That was it. Alex licked her lips and sat down on her couch and nodded her head.

"Don't make me wait, Corn Fed. Show me what you got. Let's see how your body moves off the field."

He grinned and cocked his head to the right and began to gyrate his hips to the beat of the drums. His shirt came off first. Which gave Alex a full view of his bare chest. Cane flexed his pectoral muscles as he danced. His biceps were like two solid boulders and Alex wanted to leave her seat and grab onto them and not let go. He was the kind of mountain climb she would sign up for. His body was an exotic vacation and made Alex want to call in sick and cancel her plane ticket home.

Dayum. Her eyes trailed down his stomach as she took in yes, an eight pack. Maybe that's why he skipped dessert? How many crunches did he do daily? Alex wanted to sit and watch. Maybe drizzle some water over his skin as his body moved. The idea of Cane on the floor doing crunches or even better, push-ups, cranked up the heat between her legs to lava level. It was a good thing she had something on under the t-shirt otherwise she would have made an impression of her excitement level on the couch.

Almost as if in response, Cane's pants were on the floor. Alex had tunnel vision and couldn't break the trance. His cock was erect and so big. She knew he was huge, but this was the first time she was able to take all of it in visually. Good lawd the man was beyond huge. He was like Godzilla of cocks. How could Cane even shower in front of his teammates? They must all have serious complexes around him.

"Do you want me to keep going?" Cane pulled on his

briefs as his hips moved like he was going to thrust into her from across the room. Alex's voice had been lost a long while back. Now she was the one unable to form words in her head. Like she had slipped into a previous memory and time in her life where she saw Cane as an option. And that maybe he saw the same in her. Despite the signs that were in bright red that shouted "Dead End", "Danger Up Ahead", she ignored all of them. Her brain was not going to run this play. Nope.

She nodded. Her chest was so tight like the air had been sucked out of her lungs. The apex of her thighs tingled. Cane's briefs dropped to the floor and he stood before her naked. His cock flexed to the beat. The rhythm of his body to music was too much for Alex to take in. It was the most erotic sexual thing she had ever seen in her life. This moment was one she would remember for later. It was so hot. He was so hot. Dayum. Just dayum.

Alex rubbed her lips. Cane danced his way over to her and lifted her off the couch. His lips barely grazed hers. "Did you like that, sweetheart?"

Alex ignored the question and kissed him hard. She found his tongue. She would keep it busy so he wouldn't be able to ask again. She didn't want to admit out loud how much she enjoyed it. It was obvious she had. No need to verbalize this. Besides, Cane was short on words and more on moves. Body moves. He was all physical. Nothing cerebral or frontal cortex of memories or brain matter to contend with. She was sure of this.

Cane carried her down the hallway and into her bedroom. His hands were all over her body. He pulled her shirt off as he kissed her neck down to her breasts.

A vibration buzzed on the bed next to them. Fuck. No. Alex turned over and reached across the bed to find it. God. Why now. She frantically looked for it. Cane flipped on her bedside lamp and held up her purple vibrator.

"Looking for this?" He raised an eyebrow at her.

She reached for it and he retracted his hand. "Cane, give

it to me."

"Oh, I'm going to, sweetheart."

Worse than the vibrator in this moment was a navy piece of material that was not exactly hidden on her bed. She laid down on it and smiled up at him.

He cocked his head to the right. "Alex, what are you hiding?"

"What? I'm not hiding anything. Turn the lights off. You said you were going to give it to me, did you change your mind? You're not choking in the endzone, are you?" She batted her eyelashes at him.

Cane laughed and effortlessly rolled her over. He picked up the navy piece of material with Clayburn written on the back. Alex died a slow and quiet death.

CHAPTER EIGHT

Cane felt a laugh form deep in his belly. Satisfaction, that is what he felt. She had his jersey. The smile on his face made his cheeks ache. That douche at dinner wasn't her type. Cane was. This was confirmation. Everything she said was full of nonsense. He never bought it.

"Put it on."

Alex's cheeks burned red. She shook her head vigorously. "No, I don't even know why I have that. I mean, I was about to give it to goodwill. Yeah. I was clearing out my closet."

"You were going to give my jersey and your vibrator to charity? Good story, sweetheart. I can see why you're a writer."

Alex tried to pull the shirt from his grip but Cane wasn't letting this one go. Suddenly his only desire in the world was to see her in his jersey, his name across her back, claiming her. "Put it on." He lowered his voice as he pressed his mouth against her cheek. "I want you to wear it while I fuck you."

Alex licked her lips and wordlessly complied. She tossed her shirt at the bottom of the bed. Fuck she was hot, glasses on, her hair pulled back in a messy ponytail, plain white cotton underwear. Nothing fancy, just Alex, sexy as fuck, Alex. God, he wanted her. He wanted to admire her body the way she had just admired his but he had asked her to put on his jersey and she was. Next time she would be naked. In the shower, he wanted her in the shower so he could stare at her naked breasts and work soap over her nipples until she moaned. God, he loved the sounds she made. When would he stop thinking about the next time they were going to have sex? When would he get enough? Not tonight. There were not enough hours left.

"Light is staying on," Cane warned.

"I wouldn't have it any other way." Alex's mouth puckered into a sultry smile. "I want to check out the goods, Corn Fed. You don't go to the gallery and then close your eyes."

"Turn around. I want to see my name on your back."

Alex threw her head back and laughed. "Your ego is as big as your dick." She bent over and tugged off her panties.

"Not quite."

Alex turned around then glanced back over her shoulder. "Want to take me from behind. Then you can look at your name the whole time. You'd like that, wouldn't you?"

The thought sent blood rushing to his cock. He didn't think he could get any harder but he was wrong. The thought of his name on her back turned him on more than he could have imagined, but not for the reason she thought. It had nothing to do with vanity. It was more primal than that. It was marking her, staking his claim. He wanted his name on her body. He wanted to be connected to her for more than a quickie or some over infatuated flirtatious bathroom moment.

This wasn't him, not who he was. Cane moved on as soon as he came, but not with Alex. Why? Objectively, she wasn't the most beautiful woman he had been with, but he would floor any man who dared to say that to him.

"What do you say, Corn Fed? Want me on all fours?"

Hell yeah, he did. He wanted her from behind and on

top and in the shower and on the couch while they watched highlights from the game. He was going crazy. Straight up insane. This was not normal. His reaction to her wasn't right.

Cane grabbed Alex and pulled her hard against his chest. He lifted her off the floor, her legs tangled behind him. And then he kissed her. Her mouth was soft and yielding, parting for him as he coaxed her lips open with his tongue. All thoughts faded from his mind, his desire singular: to be in her, with her, lose himself in her. This is what a kiss should be like. He could kiss her all night and still want more. There was something about Alex that was like an intoxication he never thought could consume him. He was not the one-woman kind of guy. He was a perineal bachelor. He was the guy that no one could nail down. He was the nailer and bailer. Always on the prowl never locked in. Never a commitment.

Cane laid them down on the bed. He needed to be in her. Nothing else mattered. "Condom," he whispered against her mouth.

"Top drawer."

Cane opened the top drawers, condoms in every variety, every color and flavor, size and shape. A bolt of jealousy stabbed him in the gut. *Mine.* His mind roared. Cane wasn't going to share. Alex belonged to him now. He would be using the rest of those condoms. Nobody else would be touching his woman again.

Cane tore open the packet and rolled the condom over his length.

"Last chance to get me on all fours, Corn Fed."

Cane smiled. "Not my last chance. Never my last chance. I'll have you from behind and on top and on bottom. I'm going to have you in ways you haven't even thought of yet." He pushed her back and entered her in a long fluid movement enjoying the sensation of her pussy stretching taut against him.

Alex closed her eyes and sighed. "So much better than a

vibrator." She smiled.

"That's music to my ears, sweetheart."

Alex's eyes flew open. "Stop calling me, sweetheart."

"No!" Cane thrust hard into her, pinning her to the bed. "Nope, that's not going to happen, sweetheart."

Alex opened her mouth to object but he silenced her with a kiss. She groaned an objection, but when his hand slid between them and found her clit the sound morphed into a needy moan. She was so responsive, everything he did, every move he made. Their bodies just fit. The way they moved, the way they thought, everything.

His tongue danced with hers, tasting and exploring. Her nails scratched down his back, grabbing at his ass, forcing him in deeper. She wanted more of him and he would give it to her. If she could take it, he would give it. He thrust into her further, not stopping until he hit the soft barrier of her cervix.

She moaned again into his mouth. She was about to come. He felt it in the spasms around his cock. She was so close now. Over and over, he pounded into her, not holding back. They both needed this. Alex screamed out her orgasm, the words lost in his mouth.

He thrust into her again and then came, only seconds behind her.

Cane rolled them both to their side so he would not crush her. He held her tight against his chest. Her heartbeat hard against his.

"No interceptions that time, Corn Fed." There was satisfaction in Alex's voice.

"What's my name, Alex?" Cane suddenly realized he could not remember her ever saying his name. He liked that she called him Corn Fed, it was meant as an insult but secretly he knew it was an endearment. Cane wanted to hear his name on her lips, the same way he wanted his jersey on her back.

"What? What do you mean? It's literally written on my back. Should we have done it doggy style to remind you?

That's taking the whole dumb jock thing to a new level but I'm down with it," she joked.

"I'm serious. Say my name," he demanded.

Alex's eyes narrowed. "Clayburn."

Cane smiled. "No, my first name. Clayburn could be any of my brothers. I'm not down with that. Say my first name. Please tell me you know it. You at least did that much research."

There was a familiar flash of defiance in her eyes. God, he loved that he could make her do anything with the slightest challenge. "Cane, Corn Fed, White Boy Clayburn."

Cane smiled then kissed her. "This is nice. I like your apartment. Its handy, close to the stadium." Cane rolled onto his back. He was telling her he would be back without using the words. She could fight with words, best to not open things up for an argument yet. He was still in the post sex zone. They could have that argument later.

"Thanks. It's nice, I guess. I'm not ready to buy." Alex tried to pull away from him but Cane kept her pinned against his chest. "What are you doing?"

"I'm cuddling my girlfriend after sex. It's a thing apparently."

Alex pushed against him but Cane's iron grip meant she did not budge. "Don't start that biz again. I'm not your girlfriend. Let me up. I want to watch the highlights from the Cowboy's game."

Cane kissed the top of her head, ignoring her, she wasn't going anywhere. And certainly not to watch the Cowboys. "I read that post coital cuddling fosters intimacy. So that's what we're doing."

"Stop pretending you can read. Ahh, I don't cuddle. Ever." Alex protested when he pulled her in closer.

"Yeah, me either," he admitted. This was new for him, too. "But I thought starting with my girlfriend would be the best bet. Apparently, this is the way forward for relationships."

"Ahh." Alex groaned. "You're torturing me. Seriously

what is the point of this?"

"I told you. Intimacy, baby." Cane laughed.

"Do you need a dictionary? That thing we just did was the intimate part. This part is just weird."

"Shh, you're ruining cuddle time, Alex. We're going to have to practice this until you get it right."

Alex pushed against him with all her might. Her face turned red from the exertion. Finally, she gave up. "You're such an ass."

"We'll start you off slow. Five minutes cuddle time."

"What? You expect me to lay here saying nothing for five minutes? Are you smoking crack, Corn Fed?"

Cane smiled. "You can talk, you just can't talk shit and try to get away. Time doesn't start until you stop squirming."

"Fine. Start the clock. Five minutes." Alex laid her head back down in the crook of his arm.

"See, that's nice, right? I can see why people are into this." He really could. Cuddling after sex was nice. Who knew? And why had they never told him?

"Don't push it. It's tolerable. Kind of like a trip to the dentist. It's not going to kill me but I'm not going to rush out and make another appointment."

"So how was your day? Anything exciting happen?" That totally sounded like a boyfriend question. He was in the zone. This was a whole different field for him. But he was focused on being the best. Boyfriend material was never on his scorecard but it was never too late to add to his achievements.

"Well, I went on a date with a chiropractor. Then I came home and had sex with a quarterback. And then he ruined it by forcing me to cuddle. That pretty much sums up the highlights."

"Awe. I'm a highlight." Cane kissed her temple. "Look at you getting in the girlfriend zone. You're a quick study. I think I'll have you broken in by Christmas. You'll be wanting your own drawer at my house and I'll be like, settle down, sweetheart. We only just started dating. And you'll be like but I want to have all four of your ten-pound babies."

"You are in the danger zone of ridiculousness. Hold up. You weighed ten pounds at birth?" Alex pushed back against his chest. Her eyes were wide with what most might consider fright.

"Ten-pounds and two-ounces. I was the smallest, but to be fair, I was two weeks early so still a decent enough size, I guess. I think our boys will hit eleven pounds. You look like you come from good sturdy stock." Cane grabbed her ass. It was the right amount of cushion.

"Ten-pounds! What the hell do they feed you people in Cut and Shoot that your women have ten-pound babies? That is insane. Like some mutant breed. Normal humans don't come out that big."

"You did do research. You know my hometown. Not just a pretty face. Did you figure out the other part of the story you got wrong, yet?" He scanned her face for any signs of recognition. Of any reporter he thought she would have known.

"I looked at the reels again. I was spot on."

"Sweetheart, no need to watch videos of me. I will give you a show any time you want."

"Tell me. What did I get wrong?"

"Nope."

"Please. You're killing me."

"Absolute score. I love when you beg. I will be making you do that later."

Alex groaned just as the timer on the stopwatch went off.

"Times up. How awesome are we at this couple thing? Next round we go for six minutes. And then we'll work up to spooning. That's a thing, too." He kissed her head before she could pull away.

Alex picked up a pillow and hit him. "We are not spooning. Ever. You are never sleeping over. I don't do that. I usually only play away games so I can leave right after sex."

Cane's eyes narrowed. "You never have sex in your own apartment? That's kind of weird. Why do you have all those condoms in your drawer?"

"Where else would I keep them? I have a dozen in my purse but I can't keep them all there. Now that would be weird."

"You have a lifetime supply. You know they keep making them. You can always buy more later."

"Ha! Very funny, lifetime supply. No, you're serious. Oh, Corn Fed. That drawer won't even last until the playoffs. Right there is why you will never be my boyfriend. You wouldn't be able to keep up." Alex stood up. "I'm hungry. I had to skip dessert because the guy I'm hooking up with showed up at the restaurant where I was having a date. Totally awkward."

"Good thing I brought ice cream."

"Bluebell?" Alex faced Cane with a look of desire that was different from the bedroom.

"Is there any other kind?"

"Now you're talking my language. What flavor?"

"Dulce le leche."

Alex spun around. "That's my favorite."

"I know. I told you. One of us is good at research. And it ain't you."

Cane took the ice cream from the freezer. "Spoons?"

Alex grabbed two and headed to the couch. She slid her glasses on and reached for a notebook.

"You look sexy in glasses."

Alex laughed and shook her head. "You look sexy naked. Now shh. I have work to do."

"Poor you having to watch the Cowboys. Not even if they paid me."

"Shh, Corn Fed. You just sit there and look pretty. The grownups are working." Alex stuck her spoon in the carton. "Great research by the way. Who did you call?"

"I'm not revealing my sources."

"As a journalist, I totally respect that."

"I knew you would."

Alex pushed play. Her brows knitted together as she concentrated on the screen, as she scribbled down notes. A few times she paused to have another spoonful of ice cream or rewind to watch the play again.

"Avoid that guy." Alex pointed at the paused screen. "He is a dirty player. He's going to hurt somebody. I mean, more than he has already. Eight fines in four years is crazy. I'm serious. Stop smiling at me, Corn Fed. Your left tackle is letting you down. Work on that. I mean it. Tell him. He's supposed to have your bind side. He doesn't, so God only knows what they are paying him for."

"Awe, look at you being a concerned girlfriend. And you know what you're talking about. You understand football. Fuck, that is sexy. I'm going to need to fuck you again. You're too much."

Alex laughed. "I'm working!"

"I know, sweetheart. You keep watching TV. The grownups have work to do right here." Cane set the ice cream down on the coffee table. Alex was still in his jersey without any panties.

Cane slid to the floor in front of her.

"Cane, I'm serious. I have to get this done."

She said his name. Progress. "Keep working. I wouldn't dream of stopping you. They lost just so you know. Just like they will lose when we play them."

"Only if you sort out your blindside."

"Right there is why I can't keep my hands off you. Or my mouth." Cane spread her legs apart. He lowered his head between her thighs. "I've been thinking about this since the day in your office. The way you taste. God, you have a nice pussy. Has anyone ever told you that? Cause you do. So nice." Cane's tongue glided across the seam of her body, through her dark curls to the soft pink flesh.

Alex sucked in a sharp breath. Cane spread her legs wider so he could admire her, all of her. There was no shyness, she did not struggle or ask him to stop. Fuck she was sexy. She knew what she wanted and went after it. He appreciated that. He would just have to make sure it was always him that she wanted. Good thing he was up to that challenge.

He lowered his head again. His tongue found her clit. He sucked on the swollen nub. His tongue circled her, small loops at first then licks that went all the way down to the entrance of her body. He slid his tongue into her, where his cock had just been. Her hips jerked up but his hands kept her firmly in place. There was no getting away from this, from him. In and out, Cane stroked until Alex's breath was coming in small pants.

"Oh, God! Yes." She moaned.

Cane's mouth went higher, back to her clit. He flicked it with the pointed tip of his tongue, teasing her. Alex laced her hands through his hair and pushed his head harder into her. He could stop moving entirely and Alex would come by rubbing her pussy on his face, but he wasn't going to stop. Cane was going to make her come. He sucked again.

"Oh fuck…oh my god. Right there. Don't you dare stop."

Cane had no intention of stopping until she came hard against his tongue.

Alex's hips bucked as she cried out as her orgasm washed over her. Cane kept licking until the last tremor faded and then he kissed the inside of her thigh. "Enjoy the rest of your night, sweetheart. No more dates with other guys. I don't share."

Cane picked up his keys and headed for the door. "Next time we're at my house. Pack a bag cause you're staying over so we can work on spooning. Night."

CHAPTER NINE

Alex ran through her first article about Cane again. What had she missed? He obviously wasn't going to tell her. She was going to have to figure it out for herself. America's Corn Fed Farm boy...that part was right. His nickname was smiles. She had that right. Everyone called him smiles back at UT. He'd had that moniker since he was a kid. Probably always had that big dumb look on his face. Except he wasn't as dumb as she had thought.

He challenged her and was able to deliver his own comebacks without a script. He was good at that but this could be from typical guy banter. Players are always one upping one another on and off the field. Alex had witnessed this first hand as a reporter. Her phone vibrated on her desk.

"Send me a pic."

Alex rolled her eyes and shook her head.

"Shouldn't you be practicing?"

"Taking a water break. Send me one. Come on."

"You send me one. I know you like taking selfies from all your social feeds. You're worse than a teenage girl." She had his page pulled up on one of her browser windows. Alex had only checked it out a few times this morning. Just a couple of scrolls over some of his photos. Cane almost always posted

a daily pic of himself working out. Which would then be reshared thousands of times.

"Sweetheart, I'm happy to hear you're stalking me."

Alex rolled her eyes. Before she could respond a picture popped up on her phone. Cane's lips were puckered and his hand was open. He had sent her a kiss.

"TTYL ;)"

Alex laughed. He was so ridiculous. She put her phone back on her desk.

"Hey, got a minute?" Mason Martinez knocked on the outside of Alex's door.

"Yes." She always had a minute for her boss.

"You working on a good story?"

Alex raised her eyebrows. "I'm just going over the Clayburn story, he says I got something wrong and I can't find it."

Mason nodded. "Keep looking. You did a great job with that story. Got tons of shares and reposts. Keep up that kind of reporting and you'll be moving from the papers to the screen in record time."

Alex's chest tightened. An on-air spot was every side line reporter's dream. "Will do."

"Make sure you get a quote from Clayburn tomorrow. It's the last pre-season game. If you get another good one, we'll be sending you to the away games." He rubbed his ginger-colored beard. "Ask him about Ms. Texas, whether he does good or bad. Egg him on."

Her throat constricted. Alex didn't want or need to ask what he meant but she knew there was a reason for the Ms. Texas comment. She forced herself to speak. "Why would I ask about Ms. Texas?"

Mason clicked his tongue against his teeth. "Alex, you're a reporter you should be on top of this. He was kissing Ms. Texas last night. It's all over the gossip mags."

Alex's heart squeezed tight. "Last night?" she asked.

"Yea, outside of Masraff's." He scratched his head. Like he needed to contemplate her skills. No, he did not. She was ready for on-air. She was ready for anything. Alex did not let her guard down for a second. Other than with Cane. But she would remedy it as soon as Mason left.

"Okay. I'll check that out."

"Make it a good story, Alex. You've got this."

"Yes, sir."

He turned on his heel and exited her office. Alex pulled up her search bar and Googled Cane Clayburn and Miss Texas.

Two hundred and eighty-six thousand results were two hundred and eighty-five thousand nine hundred and ninety-nine too many. Alex picked up her phone and scrolled through her contacts. Cane had typed boyfriend when he had entered his number into her phone. Edit. Scroll. Delete. Goodbye farm boy. She was right about him. It was fine. He was good in bed. They had some good sex. Scratch that. Amazing sex. But that was it. Nothing else and nothing more would come from it. He was being placed on permanent suspension. Cane Clayburn would not be going near Alex's body. Even if every single one of her fingers were broken. That sliver of what they were was now absolutely nothing. The last particle of sand had dropped into the glass and it was a reality check. He wasn't the brains she desired and she obviously wasn't the blond trophy he wanted. It was fine. She was a fool to think that time had changed either of them.

Alex put away the articles on Cane. She didn't need to figure out his mystery anymore. She would get her quote from him tomorrow and do her job. She was a professional. Her sights were set on greater heights. Being on-air. Focus on this and forget him. He is a football player. She knew this.

***

It was fifteen after six as Alex pulled her car into the garage of her apartment. She was famished. The fumes from the Chinese take-out on her passenger seat were intense. If the lo mein wasn't so messy she would have eaten it on the way home.

Inside her house she popped open her chopsticks from the paper wrapper and dug into the greasy noodles. Her phone buzzed on the table.

Alex eyed the screen. It was an unknown number. Normally she might pick up but given that she recognized this number there was no way she was going to do that. She hit the red button to decline the call. No thanks.

Her lo mein was on point. *Very tasty. Just enjoy this. Everything is fine. Good meal. Really a good day. Work couldn't be better.* She nodded to herself.

The phone vibrated and a text message popped up.

"Where are you? It's time for an away game at my house."

Alex's eyes squinted. No way. She would never step foot in his house. Even if it was for an interview. Nope. All their chats going forward would be on the field.

She placed her chopsticks down. Her appetite had disappeared. Alex sighed and tossed it in the refrigerator. The ice cream he had brought was in the freezer. She almost wanted to eat it. All of it. Instead, she put the carton in the sink and filled it up with hot water. Little chunks of caramel floated to the top. *Bye, bye sweet cream. We are through.*

Her phone vibrated on the table again.

"You better not be on a date. I was serious. I do not share."

Unbelievable. What a complete hypocrite. He really was an idiot. Did he honestly think he could hook up with other women and then show up at her house and she would be okay with that? And then all his couple conversations. What was that about? Was that a joke to him? Ah. Now it made sense. Yes, she was a joke to him. There was no way he was actually interested in her. Maybe he even knew or had figured it out and this was just some stupid game. Her eyes filled with tears. Not going there. She wiped them away.

"Alex, are you at home?"

She rolled her eyes. She pulled up her search bar on her

phone and typed in the same words as earlier. With a click of three buttons, she forwarded the photo to him. Alex did not hesitate on her next move. She turned her phone off and went to bed. Her mind had had enough for one day.

***

Piece of cake. Piece of cake. Piece of cake. Alex blew the hair off her face. After tonight's game she would reward herself with a piece of cake. A thick chocolate molten lava cake. No, she would get dulce de leche cheesecake from the Cheesecake Factory. It was a shame she had melted all that ice cream down the sink but she didn't want anything from him. Tomorrow she really would donate his jersey to Goodwill. She wouldn't throw it away but someone else could have it. Alex shivered. No. No one else could have it. Not after everything that had happened while she had worn it. No. She would just have to burn it. Yes. Burn baby burn. It was not exactly the easiest days of her life. But her focus was on her work. She was not going to let Cane come between her success and happiness. She could be happy without him that was not a problem. She just needed to get through the work part of being around him and not being bothered. At all. Alex made her way through the parking lot and into the Fan Zone. The crowd had been there since five. Obviously, Cane was there with his pen in hand. He always met with the masses prior to the game. It was a tradition. Alex worked her way through the people. She kept her head down and her eyes focused on the exit. She needed to make it out of this room without being noticed. Cane had texted her several times over the past twenty-four hours but what he had said was beyond Alex. She had deleted all of them without even a glance. He had been deleted. If he texted again tomorrow, she would block his number. Technology was on her side.

***

Cane towered over the fans as he signed various forms of memorabilia. It wasn't exactly a great move on his part. He should let his hand rest before a game. This made no sense. Well, it did, given it was Cane. Nothing about him made sense.

"Alex." His voice boomed over the crowd. "Alex." What in the world? Why was he doing this? She picked up her pace. All the fans parted as if he were a God, to allow him through to her. Alex pretended to be oblivious to his calls and made her way into the journalism booth. Distance that's all they needed. She let the door shut hard behind her. This was a player free zone. It was against NFL regulations to have a player in the press booth. There were rules and Alex knew them. She assumed Cane did as well.

"Hey Frank, how's the wife?"

"Good, when are you going to settle down? Give up the pen and make babies." He chortled.

Alex laughed. "Hilarious. If your copy was as good as these jokes your article might actually make it past page eleven."

She sat down and took out her laptop and notebook. Her focus was on the field. The announcements began with a run through of each of the Houston Texans starting line-up and the lights went out for a second before Cane came out on the field with smoke billowing behind him. He did his signature elbow thrust and the crowd went wild. Of course, they did. Cane was a star from his sandy blond hair to his chiseled jaw. His massive shoulders combined with the pads, made him seem like an actual giant. The man was enormous. In every way. The apex of Alex's thighs tingled. She bit the inside of her cheek. No. No more. That was over. She wanted an actual boyfriend that would lead to a fiancé and finally a husband. Alex was tired of dating. She wanted real love coupled with fun. Alex swallowed. *Let it go.*

The center, Stotzer, snapped the ball and Cane passed it down the field to Halfkinney. The man had speed. He caught it and made it to the forty-yard line. Not bad for the first play. The team moved down the field and set up for the next first down. Cane's eyes were focused every time the camera panned on him. His face was serious. He was in the zone. He had been in the zone with her. God, he'd been in the zone. The man knew what he was doing. *Stop. Don't think about it. Let it go.*

Three hours later the game ended with a final of twenty-three to twenty-one. Texans pulled it out with a safety. Alex made her way to the field, she had to get her quote. She blew the hair from her face. September in Houston was hot. Not like August hot, but still hot and she had on her tan blazer over her blue cami blouse. The hickey was gone, thankfully. She specially chose the blue that was more Cowboys than Texan if it wouldn't have been against regulations, she would have worn a Cowboy jersey. Anything to further the idea that she was not interested.

Cane swaggered his way toward her. His teeth reflected the lights off of the stadium and his face was full of happiness. Yes, he did a great job. Perfect. But he did get sacked twice. Alex would need to mention that.

"Hey sweetheart, you ready to talk?" He towered over her with his words and his physical presence.

Alex bit the inside of her cheek to check herself. Game on. Game face. Play this right. She pulled out her recorder and hit the red button. Let's do this.

"Great game. What were you thinking about in the last quarter?"

Cane smiled. "My girlfriend. She is really feisty. And even when the score is down, I know we'll pull through."

Alex clenched her left fist together. Focus. Ground yourself. Her smile was forced. Almost bright enough to show the falsity of it. She wouldn't give hint the satisfaction. No, she was focused, too. "That's so sweet. Is Miss Texas, please forgive me but I don't follow the pageants, so I'm not sure what her name is, but is she here tonight supporting you?" Alex batted her eyelashes at him. She could play this any way she wanted as long as she quoted him verbatim it was all good. And she would. She would quote whatever Cane said and spin it to her own benefit.

Cane stared at her while he reached out and grabbed her recorder, hitting the stop button.

"Alex, let me explain. I'm assuming you didn't read my texts?"

Alex reached for the recorder and hit the button. "As I was saying is she here tonight supporting you?" She tilted her jaw up at him. If he wasn't such a giant, it might have been perceived as condescending but that was difficult to portray with the height difference.

Cane glared at her. "My girlfriend is here tonight supporting me and I think knowing that she was here made it all the more special." He tapped his large finger over his mouth. His finger that had been inside her. Over the mouth that had licked her to the most amazing orgasm. No... Focus.

"That's great. What happened with the two sacks? Would you blame Peterson or hold yourself accountable for your own actions?"

Cane's eyes left her face for a brief second. He was good. She would give him that, but she had him where she wanted him. He wouldn't out another teammate. Ever. That was fine. Alex needed something quote worthy. *Go on Cane. Speak. Mess up. Do what you do. Choke under pressure.*

She sighed. "Well?"

"The sacks are just part of the game. Everyone knows that things happen that are not planned. Maybe someone made a poor choice and then someone goes down. It doesn't mean game over. It just means it's time for another first down." His eyes were a dark shade of blue. So dark, the color mirrored that of his uniform. She was not going there. She got her quote. Time to get out of there.

"Great. Thank you." Alex turned on her heel and made her way back toward the press booth. She needed to get her stuff and leave. She had plenty of quote worthy material and she intended on using all of it.

GIA STONE

CHAPTER TEN

Thursday. The week was almost over. Thank, God. Not that it really mattered, Alex worked weekends anyway because that is when football games were played, but she normally only let herself drink on Friday and Saturday nights. It was almost wine o'clock, even if it was a Thursday. She would be drinking to forget Cane Clayburn. A bottle of red and he would be gone. Boom. Or maybe two and then sex with a random guy. Someone hot. Someone that could really move. Someone with big hands to hold her down. *Cane. Damn it.* Basically, she wanted Cane but not Cane. Not a letdown, an ass on an easy day. That is what she wanted, a guy that wasn't an ass. So definitely not Cane.

He had texted her a dozen times since the game but she had deleted every single one before she could read them. High five. She was almost over Cane. Not that she was ever under him (other than for mind blowing sex), it was just temporary insanity. She had cock blindness. That had to be a thing, when you're delusional over a smoking hot man. Yep, that's what she had. But it was fine. He was almost out of her system.

Date number two with the dentist was on Saturday night. He had serious potential. He was on the short side but Alex would forgo heels. He was smart and easy enough on the eyes and he hated football. He would never ask for a picture with Cane Clayburn.

A knock sounded on her door.

"Come in." Alex clicked on her browser so it looked like she was busy with an article and not side-tracked with daydreams.

"You must have impressed somebody," Mason announced.

Alex raised an eyebrow. "What? What are you talking about?"

"Max Argyle has agreed to an interview. With you."

"Shut the front door." Alex stood up. "Are you kidding me? Please say you are not kidding. You can't joke about Max Argyle." Max had been Alex's idol since she was old enough to pick up the sports section and read it for herself. Max was a wide receiver with the Oilers back when they were based in Houston. He was only the best player in NFL history. And he never gave interviews. He hated journalists. He lived off the grid in Central Texas. And she was going to meet him? This couldn't possibly be true.

"No, he called this morning. Said he would give an interview but only with you. He read your article about Cane Clayburn. It made him laugh."

Alex flushed at the mention of Cane. Nope, he was not going to ruin this moment. "Are you serious? Tell me you're serious. When does he want me to call?"

"He said he wants to speak to you in person."

"No!" Alex could die now. *Take me now Lord because it's never going to get any better than this.* This wasn't just the highlight of her career. It was the highlight of her life.

"He can see you this afternoon at his ranch."

Alex grabbed her bag. "Send his address to my phone. I'm heading there right now. Oh, my fricking god."

Mason stopped her at the door. "No need. He sent a helicopter. You have a fan, Alex."

Her mouth dropped open. This was a dream. *Please don't*

let me wake up until after I have met Max Argyle.

***

Alex smiled at the helicopter pilot. He was tall and dark with broad shoulders. He looked vaguely familiar. She knew him from somewhere. Where Had they met before? She was going to ask him but his head set was on and he was flipping buttons as soon as Alex was strapped in. Alex stared out at the horizon. She had never been in a helicopter. It was loud and her whole body vibrated with the movement of the massive machine. Or maybe that was her excitement.

The skyline was beautiful as they left Houston. Golden plains stretched out for miles in every direction. This was farming country, like where Corn Fed grew up. She pushed the thought away. Cane was not going to ruin this.

They flew further until the landscape changed again. Massive pines covered the hills. It was beautiful, like something out of a story book with the trees and the winding river. She had no idea Texas would be this pretty from this height.

The pilot put the helicopter down in a clearing near a small cottage. Oh, good lord in heaven, the whole thing looked like a Thomas Kincaid painting. Seriously, he probably painted this before he died.

"Thank you," Alex shouted over the noise of the engine.

The pilot smiled. An odd mischievous grin on his full lips. She was certain she knew him from somewhere. But where? "You're welcome. He's in there. We'll see if you still want to thank me in the morning."

Alex raised an eyebrow. She was about to ask him what he meant, but he had already put his head set back on. So not the chatty type.

Alex took three deep breaths and let them out slowly before she knocked on the door. She was cool, calm and collected. Ice in her veins. Tingles on the back of her neck. She inhaled once more. *You got this.* She didn't even need to prepare questions because she had had them prepared in her mind for over a decade. Sometimes at night when she couldn't sleep, she would play out an on-air interview with Max in her mind. And now she was really meeting him. He was almost sixty now. Would she recognize him?

The door swung open.

Alex's mouth dropped open. She retracted it and gained her composure. She was a professional. Professional. Always. Despite, Cane's massive frame in the doorway. She would not overreact. No. It was possible he was also here with Max. Maybe Max wanted to have a joint interview. That was possible. She took in a deep breath. First thing a journalist does is take in the details. It's all about the details. Alex let a smile raise the corners of her mouth. as she made her way into the cottage. It wasn't large so she was able to give herself a speechless tour in under sixty seconds.

It was obvious Max was not there. Time to go. She went back outside. Unbelievable. The helicopter was gone. She let out a deep sigh. Trapped. No, she would not be trapped. Alex always had an exit plan. She had only been on two dates in the last four years where she let a guy pick her up. She was always prepared. All she needed was her phone and she could get herself out of any situation. Always.

"Alex, we need to talk."

His voice made the oxygen from her lungs evaporate. It was like she had been hit in the stomach hard. And that only happened once in real life in a kick boxing class. And once in a different moment that she had blocked out of her memories forever. Never again. She took in a deep breath. There was lots of air out here to breathe. They were in the middle of fucking nowhere. She had seen it with her own eyes. There was no road. No path leading to the cottage. This wasn't a Thomas Kincaid painting. This was like the movie Evil Dead. It was time to roll the credits because she was going to get the hell out. Alex dug through her purse and grabbed her phone. Perfect. Her phone had three bars. Good enough. It was time to leave.

Cane grabbed her escape plan with a fast swoop.

Alex opened her mouth to protest but that would mean words and she had zero words for Cane. The only time she intended her voice would be used with him would be on the field. This was nowhere near a football field which meant no dialogue. He could monologue all day long. But she would not join in.

She let out a sigh. No phone. That was fine. She didn't need a phone. On her feet were heels, not exactly the right shoes for a hike. But if that is what it took to get out of there than she would make it happen. Phones were replaceable. She would get a new one when she got back to Houston. It would probably take an hour or so to get to a nearby road, but it was plenty early. No need to be worried about the daylight and no doubt Cane would be behind her, so any animals could get to him first while she ran. Inside she laughed. This was so ridiculous.

Cane grabbed her waist and turned her around. "Alex, come on. Let's talk."

Talk. No thank you. Alex took in a deep breath. The ground was horrible for heels. They sank in the dirt with every step. It was like she was in a game of real-life pick-up sticks. Little branches and divots were everywhere. Why? Why was he doing this? This was ludicrous.

"I see you deleted my texts. Did you even read them?" He held up her phone high enough it was out of her reach.

No, she did not read them. Why would she? Alex had deleted his number and his texts. There was no point in any further discussion. This was obviously a game to Cane. He liked the challenge of her non-response. The moment she responded; his intrigue would be gone. Along with the next blond to cross his path. He was a player. He set her up and that was just plain mean. She had been so excited about the idea of interviewing Max Argyle. And now Cane had taken that away from her. Her eyes moistened. No way was that going to happen. Blink and gone. Just like she would be, as soon as she got out of this nightmare.

He cupped her face. Cane turned her chin up so their eyes would meet. He might be physically stronger than her but she had more willpower than he could even dream of. Alex closed her eyes. Perfect, now he was gone.

"Ah, now I get it. You can't handle talking to me. You're afraid. Alex, you don't have to be afraid. I want this as much as you do."

"Afraid. You can't be serious. I am not afraid of anything."

Cane laughed. "I knew I could get you to talk."

Alex took in a deep breath. Dammit. He was right. "Fine. You want to talk. Let' talk. Let's talk about how very uncool it is for you to trap me on a mountain under false pretenses."

"Hey, you're still going to get your interview." He ran his hand through her hair. The back of her neck tingled. No. She was not going there. Not again. Alex swallowed and took a step back.

"If you read your texts, you would know I arranged the interview with Max before the game, to say sorry for the misunderstanding. You are getting your interview, tomorrow at two o' clock."

Her heart rose. The idea of the interview was back on the table. It was like the Christmas that had previously been cancelled was back on.

"Really. Max Argyle has agreed to an interview? That wasn't just a ploy?" She tried to make her voice as smooth as possible. Nothing like the little girl in her mind. The squeals of delight were almost too loud for her to take and it was only in her imagination. Alex needed to play this cool and not give Cane anymore ammunition by being excited about the prospect of an interview. Clearly, he never got over the articles she had written. Was everything that happened after the locker room interview just an elaborate ruse to embarrass her? Was Cane that much of an ass?

"Max is a family friend. He owns the ranch beside Night Latch. I asked him to do me a favor and give my girlfriend an interview to get me back in her good graces because I did something really stupid."

Alex rolled her eyes. "I'm not your girlfriend."

"Then why do you give a shit if I kissed Miss Texas?"

Warmth rose to her cheeks. She wasn't expecting that question. She hadn't even asked it herself. It was a given she would be pissed. Cane hooked up with another woman hours before he had sex with her. Of course she would be pissed. What normal person with any amount of soul wouldn't be? Just because she had random hook-ups didn't mean she was okay with Cane's behavior to treat her as such. Not again. No. She would not be the doormat, or rather left at the doorstep. That was not her future. She had drawn a line in the dirt on this one. Forever. Her insides burned. What was this level of emotion that churned inside of her? It had to be the rush of the interview and cancellation and then being back on. It was the whirlwind of emotions that had obviously put her off her internal calmness.

Cane smiled. "You haven't even admitted it to yourself." He shook his head. "That's really something. I get not wanting to say it to me. You're afraid, but at least be honest with yourself." He ran his fingers through his hair. "Yes, you have an interview with Max. It will be on-air and I guarantee it will be picked up nationally. So, you're welcome."

Alex glanced at the ground. So many broken sticks covered with dirt. This was not her comfort zone. Being in the woods and being told to confront her feelings. No. She had told herself she was ready for an actual boyfriend and those next steps in life, but here in the woods with Cane? It was like she was back in junior high against the wall in the gym unable to say yes or no to the offer of a dance with Arrick Creamer. Or another moment that was even worse than that. She shook her head. The back of her neck was warm.

"You shouldn't have done that. I don't want any favors called in for me. If you had done your research, you would know I don't go by my actual last name." She wiped the loose hair off of her face. "Even though I don't want to, I use my mother's maiden name. I don't need special favors from my dad's career. I want to make it on my own."

"Alex, of course I am going to call in favors for you. This thing we're doing is a relationship. That's what boyfriends do. So, get used to it. Your dream was to meet Max Argyle so I made it happen. If I can make your dreams happen, I will. Don't ask me not to." There was a hint of joy in his deep voice.

"Did you also read that being in a relationship means not sleeping with other women? Or did you skip that part of the article?" Her chest tightened. The idea of Cane with anyone else made her sick. Why? She swallowed the possibility down. The lump in the back of her throat grew with the silence that followed her question. It was almost an eternity in pain. Pain of the delayed response. Of all times for Cane to take a moment to think about what he was going to say.

"You were on a date with another man. You left with another man. For all I knew, he was ball deep inside you at that point. So yeah, I kissed Monica. I didn't sleep with her. You are the only woman I have slept with since our first night."

"Monica. She even has a beauty queen name." Alex rolled her eyes. The lump in the back of her throat seemed to shrink, a little.

"Sweetheart, I love that you're jealous. But I'm not thrilled about the hypocrisy. You were on a date with that douche."

"Dean. His name is Dean."

"He even has a douche name," Cane joked.

Despite herself, she smiled. "He's not a douche but definitely not for me. Which is why I went home alone."

"You should not have been out with him at all."

She knew where this conversation was going and it was time to shut it down. "Maybe. It really doesn't matter. I need to leave."

Cane reached for Alex and encircled her body in his arms. "Stay with me."

"No, I have to go." She tried to wriggle out of his grasp. It was a limp attempt. Being in his arms even in protest was not bad. It was something she wasn't ready for, something that wasn't supposed to exist with him. Not him.

Cane pulled her in tighter and kissed her hair. "Alex, you know you can't make it out on those heels. The only way out is helicopter or horse."

Alex froze. "Horses. No. No, that won't work." She shook her head.

Cane laughed. "It will. Just like us. You're going to get over being mad and enjoy riding a horse."

Alex snapped her head round to look at Cane. He looked far too pleased with himself, beyond his usual cocky, I-have-a-big-dick swagger. "I might not be mad but I still need to leave. We've talked, now give me my phone so I can call Mason and have the pilot sent back."

"He's not coming back," Cane said simply.

"You don't know that." Alex scrolled through her contacts until she found Mason. Thank God they had cell reception up here.

"Today is his day off. He only picked you up as a favor to me. Right about now he is out in the pool with his family."

"You know the pilot, too? Of course, you do."

"Yep, that's my brother Colt."

"Your Mama was really into alliteration, wasn't she?" Alex shook her head. "Why? Why did you bring me here."

"So, we can talk."

"We've talked. I'm ready to go now."

"And, so I can make you come again. Hard enough to forget you're pissed." He pulled her in close. The aroma of testosterone, arrogance, and a woodsy balm ran through her nostrils. She inhaled as if she could not be taken under by his scent. His pheromones were no match for her willpower. She was sure of it.

"Well, that's not going to happen." Alex pointed her finger into Cane's chest. She was going to really go all in on her willpower and prove to him that she had more self-control than he could possibly conceive.

"Challenge accepted." Cane's full lips hitched into a smile.

"No, Corn Fed. It's not going to happen because I am not going to have sex with you."

Cane's smile deepened. "Already at that point in our relationship. For most people it takes marriage and a couple of kids to get to that level but we made it. We're advanced. Look at us, nailing this."

He was so smug. And arrogant. And sexy. Don't go there. Not sexy, just an ass. Alex turned away. This made no sense. Why was he doing this?

She let out a deep sigh. Alex pulled the pony tail holder from her hair then bent over and shook her hair upside down. He was in her head and her chest. Cane was in. He did not belong but he was there and she needed to get him out. She shuddered.

"Are you alright?"

"No." Alex squeezed her shoulders up toward her ears. "I will feel better when you stop pretending that what we're doing is a relationship. Stop pretending you're my boyfriend. Stop pretending—"

"I'm not pretending, Alex. We are in a relationship. I am your boyfriend."

Chills ran over her arms. "Why?" She swallowed hard. "Why do you want to pretend to be my boyfriend?"

Cane let out a stream of air. "I have no idea. But I do. I want to do this. You and me, it's on."

"Why? Why me?"

Cane smiled down at her. He had closed the gap between them. Heat radiated off his body. God he was sexy. Everything about him. She had to look away so she would not be tempted to touch him. "Is this the part where you want me to compliment you and tell you all the reasons I think you're sexy?"

Alex shook her head. "No. Now is the part where you admit that you only *think* you want me because I'm a challenge. If I stop running, you'd stop chasing. It's who you are."

"Is that why you run? So, I will chase? Stop running, Alex. See what happens. I dare you."

She made an exasperated sound. She could never resist a dare. But this time she would. "No."

"For the record, sweetheart. You will always be a challenge because that's who *you* are. We will be old and grey, sitting in our rockers surrounded by our five kids and twenty grandkids and you will still challenge me."

"Four. Four kids, Corn Fed. You are having four kids with your poor long-suffering wife who will never be me."

"Five. We are having five kids now. I added an extra baby because you pissed me off. Every time you really piss me off, we have another baby. Soon we'll have enough for our own TLC show. But we won't home school or have a church in our living room because that is some crazy shit."

Alex smiled. "Don't. Don't do that. Don't make me laugh. I don't want to date you, Cane. Dating leads to marriage and I don't want to marry you just as much as you really don't want to marry me."

"Six. Six kids now. Stop telling me what I want. I want you. I want to see where this goes. So, stop getting in your own way and let it happen."

Alex turned away and stared out over the horizon. She focused on how beautiful the landscape was so she would not focus on how beautiful Cane was. This was not an argument either one of them was going to win, so there was no point engaging any further. She would do the interview and go home. Nothing will have changed; except she would have met Max Argyle. Max "living legend" Argyle. A rush of excitement swept over her.

Alex snapped her head around. "How did you know Max Argyle is my hero? And that I am not a fan of horses."

Realization struck her. Cane knew a lot about her, things that weren't on her official bio.

"I told you, sweetheart, I'm great at research."

"That's not an answer. Who did you talk to?"

"Just a few people. To find out your favorite ice cream, I asked your secretary. Your dad told me about the horses and Max Argyle."

"You what? You called my dad for research!" Blood pounded in her ears.

"Nope, I took him to lunch."

"You did what? You better be joking, Corn Fed." Alex had never introduced any guy to her dad. She would eventually, when she found the one. Cane Clayburn was not the one. He was a guy she had hot sex with. Her dad didn't need to know about that. "Tell me you're joking."

Cane shook his head. "I'm not joking about meeting your dad or about us. Yeah, it started off as a joke but it feels right. I'm not laughing anymore."

"I think you'll find I never thought the girlfriend bit was funny. But seriously, you met my dad?"

"Yes. Why is that so hard to believe? I flew to Oklahoma and we had lunch. I hold him I was serious about you and if he saw us in the papers together, not to worry because I'm not jerking you around."

Alex rubbed frantically at her temples. If that conversation really happened, it was the deepest thing her father had ever discussed regarding her private life. Her dad didn't do emotions or anything remotely girly. When her period started when she was twelve, he handed her a box with a book to explain puberty and a package of maxi pads. He kept the bottom shelf in her bathroom stocked after that, presumably so she never had to ask him. When she was sad, she got a pat on the back. When she was excited, she got a high five. That was their level and it worked well for them. Cane had no right to rock the boat. "What did he say?" Alex asked tentatively. She wasn't sure she wanted to know the answer.

"Dad stuff." Cane smiled, refusing to elaborate.

"What does that mean?"

"It means your dad loves you and he wants to make sure you are looked after. That's it. I'm not telling you anything else because it was a private conversation. Call him. He can tell you what he said if he wants to."

Well, that was never going to happen. Alex had spoken to her dad this morning and he had not mentioned it. If he had wanted to have a heart to heart, he would have done it by now. "You are not only arrogant but also a stalker." Alex let out a laugh.

"I wouldn't have to stalk you if you talked to me."

"Or I could post everything on my twitter feed like you, so all my adoring fans can ooh and ahh over my huge biceps."

"Why do you never ooh and ahh over my biceps?"

"Because I've seen your cock. That's your real ooh and ahh body part, Corn Fed."

"Well, I will have to get that out for you to ooh and ahh over." Cane pulled her in for a kiss. He lifted her off the ground so their lips were level and carried her back into the cottage and into the bedroom. Besides being an utterly swoon worthy moment, she didn't have to tip toe through the dirt and sticks in her heels. He had made her a path without any issues. Cane had taken away the difficulty of heels and dirt. Did he realize this? Did he really want to have an actual relationship with her, one that existed beyond skin deep?

Could she let Cane in? The idea frightened her. He was scary. Not his size. That she could handle, it was the emotions. He pulled on something deeper that she wasn't sure she was ready for. It had a huge caution sign in front of it. Maybe six years ago...but now didn't seem like a possibility. Time had passed but that day hadn't disappeared from her memory.

Cane kissed her and unbuttoned her shirt. "It's gone."

"Yes, finally. Don't do that again. It's a turn off for other guys."

"There will be no other guys," Cane growled in her ear.

Alex laughed and bit at his neck. Maybe she should mark him. But not where a camera would see it. No, someplace underneath his shirt or his leg. Yes, she would have to mark his leg later. Right now, she needed him inside of her. Despite the big red do not enter. Stop. Halt. Caution. Cease. Blockade. Barricade. Alarm. Alex had a thesaurus full of words to describe what she should do. Get out now. This wouldn't end well. Despite all of this Alex erased those red flags from her mind and let her other organs speak for themselves. This was something she wanted. It was something she needed. To connect with Cane on a physical level and not simply because it was hot sex, it was deeper than that on a philosophical level. He brought her to this enhanced place and it made no sense that this corn-fed farm boy football player could bring this level of intellectual stimulation and emotional response.

Cane trailed his mouth along her neck as he unhooked her bra. His hands grabbed onto her nipples and she tilted her head back.

"No more." He lowered his head and took her nipple into his mouth until his teeth grazed the tip.

She leaned forward and undid his shirt. Two could engage in nipple intensity. She pinched on his nipple and he released hers. Their mouths met again. Cane laid her down on the bed and his eyes bore into hers.

"If you were a football player, I think you would be a running back."

"I would never play football. I like watching that's it." She tugged on his pants. "Now, I want to watch you. Give me a show."

"Sweetheart, I've already given you a show. Next one is all you."

She smiled. "You don't have to dance. I just want to see you perform. Give me the goods, Corn Fed."

"Yes, definitely a running back. You're always avoiding

the tackle. But don't worry you can't run forever. A running back's career shelf life is short." He unzipped her skirt and inched it over her hips then removed his own pants. Dayum, would she ever tire of this view? No. It wasn't possible. He was the perfect specimen. His thighs were massive. She couldn't grip both hands around them if she tried. If the desire to have him deep inside of her wasn't so incredibly strong she would have taken her time and licked her tongue over his biceps and then on to his pectoral muscles. Every time she gazed at his photos, she wanted to do that. But there was no patience left between the apex of her thighs. She needed him now.

She needed him inside of her and she wanted to grip onto his shoulders and not let go. If it were possible to have him in every day and night, she would sign the contract. She didn't want it to be a temporary fling. A one season option. No. Don't go there. Stop. This is like a scrimmage not the real deal. Take it as absolutely incredible sex and some fun chats. Yes, that's it fun chats.

"I don't have a condom." Alex suddenly realized. Shit. She always packed condoms. Always. But not today. Funny enough she didn't think she would need any when she was conducting an interview with a sixty-year-old man.

Cane grabbed his pants from off the floor and reached into his pocket. "Here. These are my results. I had the team doctor print this out and sign it. No HIV or Hep A, B, or C. And my blood type is A positive so we need to find out if you're rhesus negative before we have our first baby." He winked at her. So cocky. And so incredibly sexy.

She rolled her eyes. "It's a good thing your head isn't the only big thing on your body…otherwise I'd be out of here."

"No, you wouldn't. You're going to tire of running and I would tackle you."

"Quarterbacks aren't supposed to tackle."

"Sometimes they have to."

Alex squinted her eyes. "That's not a wise move."

"It is when you are saving the ball."

"From a fumble?" She grabbed his cock and began to stroke it. Could he have a football discussion while she worked him over?

Cane's lips formed a tight circle as his chest muscles flexed. "From anything." His eyes cut from hers down to his cock.

It was so big. She couldn't grasp the entire thing with one hand.

"Quarterback makes the calls and protects the ball."

Alex ran her hands on his balls. "But you don't want to protect your balls anymore?"

Cane flashed a wicked grin. "I'm clean, Alex. Are you?"

"Yes."

"Are you on birth control? You don't seem like someone that ever leaves things to chance."

Alex squinted her eyes at him. "Yes, I get the depo shot. No pills or periods. High five on that action." She raised her hand up to him.

Cane grabbed her hand and brought it down onto him. "I'm serious about what I said about wanting to try. This is new for me, too. I've never had a real girlfriend or had sex without a condom. Got to say I am really looking forward to that. So, brace yourself. We're going into overtime tonight."

"You seem to have a thing for overtime." She stroked his cock.

"Who doesn't like extra time on the field?"

Alex laughed. "Can't argue with that."

"Alex, I want to feel you from the inside without a condom. No barriers. In fact, I want you to get rid of your condom drawer."

"Why that would be a waste." She squinted her eyes.

"No, you are done with condoms and when we are married you can get off the shot. You're not getting any younger."

"Okay, Corn Fed. We'll see about that."

Cane flipped her over on to her back.

"Sweetheart, there are no doubts. It is a guarantee." His lips trailed over her neck and down to her breasts. He sucked on her nipples as his fingers ran over her clit. He circled them round and round with the right amount of intensity. She bucked her hips to his rhythm. He worked his mouth over to her other nipple as if he wanted to make sure he gave each one time on the clock. Over and over, he sucked until her chest tightened and her stomach muscles clenched. The pleasure flowed down and tingled through to her thighs and into her calves. Her toes curled as the orgasm vibrated through her body. Yes. God, yes. That was good. Without warning he slammed inside of her. Alex's body had a whiplash of pleasure as he pounded into her. He didn't ease in as if he needed to make sure she could take all of him. She could and he didn't hold back. He thrust deeper into her. Alex's breast jiggled against his chest. Every time their skin brushed against each other her nipples were on fire. They were so hard.

"Sweetheart, we are going to work on your flexibility. We'll take it in strides. Long strides here." He trailed his fingers over her forehead. "And right now, here." He lifted her leg up and threw it over his shoulder. His eyes met hers and he slammed into her.

Alex cried out. Her calf was on his shoulder. It was hot and she couldn't breathe. Like his cock had reached past her cervix and was about to touch the roof of her mouth. Her eyes had long since shut, or were they? She had no idea the only thing in front of her was a mirage of glitter and bright colored spots that danced through the air.

"Cane, oh my, I caaan't see." Alex's voice struggled to make its way past her lips. His cock was in so deep she was going to pass out. The ripple of pleasure began in the back of her head a sensation of ten thousand prickles that popped up and cascaded down her neck and through to her shoulders. Icy pin pricks swarmed over her arms and skated along her legs. Her thighs shook. Her entire body trembled over and over in a repetitive motion until it hit her toes. It was like an explosion of lava that radiated through her. She was done.

CHAPTER ELEVEN

Cane pulled Alex against his chest. He loved this part. Who knew? But he loved to just hold her. If he had any self-control at all he would spend an entire night just holding her against him. She fit. They fit together.

Alex pulled back. Her eyes were hooded with satisfaction. "We're wasting daylight, Corn Fed. So, unless you want an instant replay, we need to get up."

Cane glanced down at his watch. "Almost Alex, you almost had it. Three minutes and forty seconds. You were on the ten-yard line and you fumbled. Hard."

"What? That was five minutes. I counted down. I demand a booth review."

Cane tapped his watch. "It's the official time piece of the NFL, the clock ain't lying. You choked, sweetheart."

"Nope. I am still laying down. The ball is still in play."

Cane laughed. "The balls are definitely not currently in play."

"Ha!" Alex swatted his chest. "I'm serious, all this still counts. Clock is still ticking."

Cane kissed her temple. "Nope. This is not a cuddle anymore. The moment you opened your mouth it became a post-coital discussion which is nothing like a cuddle.

So…you lost."

"No. I am still in the cuddle position. And you can't be the referee and the opposing team."

"I like to think we're on the same team and I'm the MVP."

"No buddy, your award would be rookie of the year." Alex laughed "Next time," she tapped her finger into his chest, "we are going for seven minutes. Seven, Corn Fed. I am going to bring you to your knees with my cuddling. Watch me win with a safety."

"I look forward to a rematch." Cane stood up and put on his pants. He would rather stay in bed with her but they did have other things to do, like eat. He was starving. He handed Alex the travel bag he had packed for her. "Shopping for a woman is hard. She's that big," Cane demonstrated with his hands, "is not a size. So, I had to guess. The sales woman at Nordstrom was helpful. She told me not to forget makeup if it is an on-air interview. I told her you're gorgeous and didn't need makeup but she assured me that you would not thank me if I let you go on camera without foundation. What the hell is foundation? You're doing an interview not building a house. Anyway, Stacey at the Clinique counter picked all the colors. I just showed her your picture on my phone and gave her my credit card."

Alex sat up. Her hair fell over her shoulders, and onto her nipples. "You bought me clothes and makeup?"

"The other option was breaking into your apartment and getting your stuff for our first away game together. The shopping seemed like the less creepy option. Good call?"

Alex shook her head and laughed. "No! Bad call. Very bad call."

"So next time break into your apartment?"

"Next time don't kiss a beauty queen."

"Sweetheart, I'm not kissing anyone but you. Now get up. We are going for a ride."

Alex grimaced and then quickly covered for it with a tight smile. She was scared of horses but it was obvious, she would never admit it. During the season, Cane lived in Houston or in hotels around the country but whenever he got a chance he came home. He was even considering building a house here. Horses came with the territory. It wasn't a deal breaker if Alex didn't go riding with him, but he wanted her to. He wanted to do everything with her.

Alex opened the bag and examined the clothes and makeup. "Wait, hold up. You have a picture of me."

"Duh, on my phone. You're my girlfriend. You also have your own ringtone because that's a thing. Read that, too."

Alex laughed. 'Seriously, Corn Fed, stop pretending you can read. We both know I am not in this for your brains."

"By the way, I have never actually heard the ringtone because you never call me." Cane leaned over and kissed her. "Come on, time to get back in the saddle. One bad experience should not ruin a good thing. And this is a good thing."

Alex's eyes narrowed. She bit into her lip as she glanced down at the worn wooden floorboards like she was debating what to say. A small furrow formed between her brows. "Do you mean...are you talking about...are you being allegorical?" she asked. Her eyes met his briefly then cut to the floor.

"Allegorical. Nice. You are using the thesaurus I got you. But no, no allegory. I mean literally you need to get back on the horse."

Alex's shoulders slumped. She studied the floor again like the grooves were the most interesting things she had ever seen. She wasn't talking about horses. This was something else.

"What did you think I meant?"

"Nothing...and there are seventeen words that you highlighted, by the way." She tapped his chest.

"Such a great number." A grin crossed his face. "How long did it take you to find them?"

Alex laughed. "I didn't have to find them. I knew it would be your number."

"That's what I said. It is a good number."

Alex was lying about allegory. Clearly, she was talking about something else. But he knew her well enough to know she wouldn't say anything, even if he challenged her. Whatever she was thinking about she had shut down hard.

She plastered a tight smile on her face. "Let's do this. This place is too small for your ego." She pulled on a new shirt over her bra.

"If you really don't want to do this, we don't have to. Your dad told me you were bucked off at a birthday party when you were a kid."

Alex brushed past him. "He told you that when you were at lunch? How exactly does that even come up? How long were you out?"

Cane shrugged. "A couple of hours." He picked up the bag he had packed and led them around the back to the small barn where Buckles and Frankie were waiting. Buckles was the gentlest creature on the planet, mostly because she was so lazy. There was no way she would have the effort to buck anyone off.

"Seriously. You talked to my dad for a couple of hours? What did you have to talk about? My dad is not chatty. He is the strong silent type."

"Football mostly, and you. Ready?" Cane laced his fingers together to make a step.

Alex's eyes focused in determination. She was scared but she wasn't about to show it. God, he liked that about her. She just got on with things. He had no doubt she could handle just about anything life threw at her.

Alex sucked in a sharp breath as Cane helped her into the saddle then handed her the reigns.

"You, okay?"

Alex nodded. Her face was turning red. "You need to breathe."

She nodded again. "I've totally got this."

Cane smiled. She didn't but he loved that she would pretend. He swung into the saddle. "Pull this side to go left, this side to go right. Pull back to stop. But she won't need to do much of that. Buckles stops a lot on her own. Just go with it."

Alex followed him out of the barn. The path down the mountain was too narrow to ride side by side so he let Alex go first so he could watch her and make sure she was doing okay. He wished he could see her face but her shoulders told him enough, they were hitched high, close to her ears.

"You got this," he reminded her.

"Yep, I got this," she said, her voice only slightly shaking.

It took almost an hour to make their way down the mountain and into a clearing in the woods. They could have made it safely in ten minutes but Cane didn't want to push it. As they worked their way down the winding path, Alex's shoulders lowered and she settled into the saddle.

He didn't try speaking to her on the way down. She was using all her concentration to stay in place. She hadn't yet realized they would make it to the bottom no matter what she did. Once they were in the field, Cane rode up beside Alex. Her face was red but she was smiling. "So?" Cane asked as he helped her down off the horse.

"Not horrible but not something I want to do again soon."

"Well, we do need to get back."

"Nope, I'm good."

Cane led the horses down to the pond. It was a hot day for September, even by Texas standards. He let them drink and then tethered them to a tree. Alex stood at the edge of the pond, staring longingly out over the water.

"Want to swim?"

The corners of her mouth pulled up. "Yes, but I didn't bring a suit because, right now, I should be at my desk looking at your Twitter feed and pretending to work."

Cane stripped off his shirt. "No need to cyber stalk me today, sweetheart."

"Why are you taking your clothes off?"

"Cause we're going swimming."

Alex shook her head. "No suit. No swim. I play by the rules."

"I'm the quarterback I make the calls. We're swimming."

Alex shook her head.

"I have seen more of your body than your gynecologist. Let's not pretend to be shy, Alex."

"I'm not being shy."

"But you want to go swimming?" Cane's eyebrows raised.

Alex shrugged and nodded her head.

"Well, there is only one thing to be done about that." Cane wrapped his arms around her and picked her up. He threw her in the water and then jumped in after. Other than his shirt, they were both fully clothed.

"Cane Clayburn!" Alex screeched when her head broke through the water. Her hair dripped. "Why did you do that? I told you I didn't want to go in."

Cane tread water beside her. "No, sweetheart you said you wanted to swim but couldn't because of some bullshit excuse. You wanted something but you wouldn't let yourself go for it. I was giving you some allegory, baby. You got to jump in with both feet."

Alex smiled broadly. "I already thought you were the sexiest guy I have ever met and then you used a four-syllable word correctly. You're making me swoon hard, Corn Fed."

"Big words, huh? That is your thing. I could have sworn it was big cocks."

Alex swam to him. "Ooh I like those, too."

"Good thing I have both."

"Yep, good thing."

Alex swam to the side. Her clothes clung to her as she got out. "For future reference, if you want to get me naked, just ask." Alex stripped off her shirt and laid it on a rock to dry. Her underwear and pants were next. "My shoes better dry."

"I'll buy you a new pair. I'm good for it."

Alex laughed "I know. I wrote about your obscenely large contract. Bigger than the GDP of a small country."

Cane stepped out of the pond and stripped the rest of his clothing off. "You got the research about my paycheck right. Good to see you have your priorities." He laid his shoes and socks beside hers.

Alex laughed. "Let's not pretend that I am using you for anything other than your body."

"You're welcome to my body, sweetheart." His mouth hitched in a smile.

Cane laid out the blanket he had packed. They would just have to lay naked in the sun until their clothes dried, worse ways to spend an afternoon.

Alex joined him on the blanket. "I have gone over the reels a lot. What did I get wrong?"

Cane shook his head. "I've already given you my body, woman. You're not getting my secrets, too."

Determination settled on her soft features. "Oh, I'll get your secrets, Corn Fed. Every single one." Alex reached out and stroked him. Instantly his cock went hard in her hand. She tried to wrap her fingers around his girth but they wouldn't stretch. She lowered her mouth until it hovered just above the head. "I'll take an inch for every secret you tell me."

"Sweetheart, I don't have enough secrets to cover the whole thing."

Alex didn't respond, she was already sucking. Her mouth was hot around the tip. Her tongue swirled around the sensitive ridge. She knew what she was doing. Fuck did she know. Cane took in a sharp breath so he could concentrate. She licked and sucked while her hand massaged the spot just below his balls. The pressure added to the exquisite sensation. Yes, she definitely knew what she was doing. Oh, fuck yes! He would come in less than five minutes if he didn't hold back. Her head lowered just a fraction, taking him deeper. Oh god…he laced his fingers through her wet hair.

Alex pulled back. "That was a teaser. If you want me to keep going, you know what you need to do." She continued to stroke him to stoke the fire but not enough to get him off. Yep, she knew what she was doing.

"Ask nicely," he replied hopefully.

"Nope."

"Tell you you're pretty?"

Alex moved her hand away. "Tell me what I got wrong and I will keep going. And I will bring my A game. Trust me, you'll be giving *me* the MVP."

Cane groaned. He had no doubt he would be. She was good. Just thinking about her mouth on him was enough to keep him hard for the foreseeable future. Now was not the time for discussions. He needed to come hard and them make her come harder. Maybe then they would talk about it, but probably not. It was not a discussion he wanted to have with her. "We'll talk after," he said, careful not to commit to disclosing anything.

"If you ever want any part of you in any part of me, we'll talk now."

Cane swallowed. She wasn't going to let it go. "My nickname: Smiles, you got that wrong. You said it was because I always had a dumb goofy smile. That's not it." Cane didn't bother asking her to keep going because the erection was gone. His body knew where the conversation was headed.

"Why do they call you smiles?"

And there it was, the question he had hoped to avoid. He wasn't embarrassed but he hated when it became an issue, when people apologized or overcompensated. He took a deep breath. "I was born with a cleft palate. My smile was wider, so that is where the name came from. It stuck even after I had surgery to correct it."

Alex's eyes widened. A look of mortification darkened her face. "I'm sorry."

There they were: those words. There was no need for anyone to be sorry. He had been born a little differently, there were some things that had to be fixed and they were. It had absolutely no impact on his daily life. It was part of his past, not anything he still had to deal with or focus on. The nickname was really the only thing that remained. Cane shifted. "Don't worry about it."

Alex shook her head. "No that was really irresponsible of me. Kids look up to you. I don't want anyone thinking that it is something to be mocked. Not cool. I'm sorry for that. I should have done better research."

Relief eased into him, not shifting, but it's tight hold loosening. "So, you're not sorry I had a cleft pallet? Just that you misreported it?" Cane asked tentatively, holding his breath while he waited for her answer.

"It's hardly held you back, has it? You're still the most gorgeous and arrogant man I have ever met. It's all good. And plus think of all the other kids born with a cleft palate, you gave them another reason to admire you. Can your ego handle all of the adoration?" Alex laughed.

There was more he needed to tell her, the part that might apply to her sometime in the not-too-distant future. "My kids," he purposefully did not say "our" because this was about him, what he brought to the genetic table, "will all have a five percent chance of being born with a cleft palate."

Alex didn't say anything. He could not read her. Her face was expressionless. Fuck had he scared her off? Damn it. "But if they do, it is pretty easy to fix." He paused for a second. "Or abortion is an option. You can see on the ultrasound early enough." There, he had said it, everything that needed to be said. His cards were on the table. Time for Alex to show hers. Based on the look on her face, he wasn't sure he wanted to know her hand.

Alex recoiled. She held up both hands, anger and mortification radiated off of her. "No! What? Why would anyone abort their baby because of a cleft palate? If your baby has a problem, you get them help. You don't abort them. No. Just no."

Cane let go of the breath he was holding, all of the

reservations he had about Alex left with that stream of air, replaced by something else. He wasn't even sure what it was. "So, you wouldn't have an abortion if you found out the baby had a cleft palate? A lot of people do, you would be given that option no questions asked." He just wanted to make sure, before the new feeling he had for her was able to take root and grow. Unlike the horses, this was a deal breaker.

"No, of course not. Please don't ask me that ever again. Never. I could never do that. I don't care what anyone else does but if I make a choice to have a baby, I'm going to be all in."

"Jumping in with both feet, are you?"

Alex nodded. "Yes, with a baby I would. If, and that is a big if, I decided to have a baby, I am going to fully commit. It stops being about you when there is a little person involved. You can't be selfish. You need to think about them." Her eyes went dark as she looked out across the water.

Cane put a hand on the small of her back. "You're thinking about your mom, aren't you?"

Alex bit into her lip and nodded. "I know it's not her fault she got sick, depression is an illness. I know that. In my mind I do. But...I don't know."

"Tell me," he coaxed.

"I wish she had been stronger. I...god....I've never told anyone this. I blame her. I do, for not being strong. I would have been stronger. I would have fought to get healthy for my baby." Alex scrubbed at her face. "Or at least I hope I would. I don't know. Maybe it's not something you can fight. I don't know. I am just talking crap. Ignore me. I promised you a blow job and you're going to get one."

She turned to him and smiled but it didn't reach her eyes. The conversation was too much emotion for her so she was going to try to shut it down. But Cane wouldn't let her. Not yet.

"You would, Alex. You would fight it. I have no doubt

you would fight and win. Even if you get postpartum depression, you would beat it. You won't do what your mom did. Is that what you're worried about?"

Alex picked up a blade of grass and rubbed it between her fingers. "I don't know. Maybe. I don't want to do that to a baby. I love my dad so much...but I needed a mom. She took that away from me." There was a sliver of glass that covered her eyes. If she blinked, it would shatter against her lashes and let the emotion she held too closely inside to slide down her face.

Cane wrapped his arms around her. "I know. Everybody needs a mama, but it's hardly holding you back." He used the words she had. She was so fragile. Against all her tough independent energy, there was a little girl that felt abandoned. He wanted to hold her tight forever so she would never have that sadness in her eyes.

Alex nodded. She leaned forward and ran her finger over his top lip, tracing the contour. "I love your smile, by the way. Those are some kissable lips." She pushed him down against the blanket and climbed on top to straddle him. She lowered her head and licked the path her fingers had just traced. "Your kids will be lucky to get such big lips," she whispered against his mouth.

A bolt of desire shot through him. Cane wanted her, more than he ever had. He needed to be inside her. He reached between them and guided his cock to the entrance of her body then pulled her down hard until she had taken all of him. She surrounded him, hot and wet, accepting all of him.

Alex's eyes widened, unprepared for the sudden invasion. Next time he would take her slow, make it last, make sure she was ready. This time he needed to be in her, to get lost in her. It went past desire, something more primal, more demanding. He needed her.

Cane forced himself to wait until she had time to adjust but when she shifted her hips, all resolve faded. Cane held her hips as he pumped into her. His pace was fast, his thrusts demanding, he needed to be closer, further, deeper.

Alex matched his speed, her hips moved against his in a perfect rhythm. She cried out his name when she came. Cane held her in place as he pumped into her, over and over until he climaxed.

Alex collapsed down on his chest. Her heart beat against his skin, racing. Cane ran his hand down her back. She kissed his chest above his heart. There was no need to check his watch. Alex cuddled him without protest. Something had changed between them—deepened. She had to have felt it too.

***

Cane asked if Alex wanted him to stay for the interview but she said absolutely not. He knew that would be her response. Alex was single minded and focused at the best of times but when she was working, she took it to another level. Nothing and nobody were going to be distracting her. He dropped her at Max's house where the crew was already setting up for the interview.

Cane headed to the Night Latch to see his family. Cheyenne greeted him at the door, Garron toddled behind her.

"He's walking." Cane smiled at his nephew as he swept him up in his arms.

"He's running. And I'm chasing."

That sounded familiar. Cane was a bit too familiar with that dynamic, but hopefully the corner had been turned on that front. Garron had crumbs on his mouth, which he promptly wiped on Cane's shoulder and laughed. "Graham crackers, buddy. Nice. Thanks for sharing."

"When is your girlfriend coming? I am so excited to meet her." Cheyenne stood on her tiptoes and kissed his cheek. He had known Cheyenne his entire life and his brother Colt had loved her just as long.

Girlfriend. Cane hadn't used that word with his family

but it was pretty obvious. He had never brought a woman home, ever, not to Cut and Shoot, and certainly not to meet his family. And he had brought her to the cottage where Colt had brought Cheyenne and Case had brought Jamison. Yeah, it was pretty obvious.

"I think she will be here by four o'clock."

"Perfect. That will give me time to get to know her before your mama gets here. I'm going to bottom line it for you. Your mama is not a fan. She read both articles. I will sit them at opposite ends of the table. It will be fine. I will put Jamison beside your mama. She loves him. He is a good buffer." Her tone sounded less than convinced.

"Lots of articles have been written about me." Cane shrugged. He focused his attention on Garron who was now pulling books out of a shelf.

"And I pity every one of those people, too." Cheyenne took a book from the baby's hands and placed it on a higher shelf. "It will be fine. But just in case, I'm not giving either of them knives." Cheyenne flashed him her best Country Darlin smile.

***

Cane played with the baby while Cheyenne started dinner. Garron looked just like Colt, with his warm brown eyes, but the baby had sandy hair like Cane and Cord. Cheyenne wasn't kidding when she said the kid liked to run. Cane was getting an extra workout in. Garron squealed when Cane swooped him up and tossed him in the air. This is what he wanted; a family of his own. His football career wouldn't last forever. He had made enough to retire after he played out his contract. He loved it, though. He would play as long as he could.

His phone vibrated in his pocket. A message from Alex.

"Thank you for the interview. Please apologize to your family. I can't make dinner tonight. Flying to Oklahoma to see my dad. He's sick. Nothing major but I want to make sure he eats. Sometimes he

forgets during the season. Thanks again, Corn Fed."

Cane messaged back. *"Do you want me to come with you?"* He could fly to Oklahoma and back before the game to spend time with Alex.

Two minutes later, a response came. *"No. You're already too into me. If you come, you'll be picking out China patterns and looking at engagement rings. Better call a time out and get some time on the bench."*

Cane laughed as he typed. *"Already picked it out. See you on the sidelines, sweetheart."*

CHAPTER TWELVE

The flight from Houston to Oklahoma City took less than an hour and a half. Alex's dad would be at the bar. He always waited in the bar. Beer and nuts while he ran over plays in his notebook. He still used pen and paper. No matter how many electronic devices Alex gave him he refused to progress into the idea of technology. She made her way down the escalator. From her viewpoint the back of his head was easy to pinpoint. Yup. His hair was less and less full each year.

"Hey, Dad." Alex tapped him on the shoulder.

"Alexandra." He tipped his cheek for her to kiss. That was the extent of their warm reunion. It had been several months since she had visited but it didn't matter, her dad was not giddy and he didn't do hugs.

He took her backpack and slung it over his shoulder. "You fly back tomorrow?"

"Yea, I don't want to risk anything and I'll be reporting live on Sunday."

"How about that? Did Cane arrange that interview for you?" He clicked the remote and they both got into the Suburban. It was maroon. Everything that could have a color choice was maroon for her father. He had coached for the University of Oklahoma for twenty years.

Alex squinted her eyes. She wanted her dad to be proud of her on-air interview. "Yes, apparently Max is a neighbor of his parents. I asked him not to call in any more favors for me."

"That's a nice favor. Max Argyle never gives interviews."

"I know." Alex took in the view. It was similar to Houston but not as big. They drove up to the circle drive in front of the twelve thousand square foot house. Home sweet home. Alex's chest tightened. Had Cane been here? No, they had gone to lunch. Probably Ray's BBQ, her dad loved their brisket.

They made their way into the house and Alex headed for her room. Everything was the same as the day she left for college. Her dad wasn't happy about her choice but UT had a better journalism school than OU. Everyone knew that. She dropped her book bag on her bed and logged onto her laptop. Fifteen emails flashed up at her. She scanned through them.

"Great job! The network wants to meet with you tomorrow at 3 p.m. -Mason"

Alex's eyes bulged out from their sockets. Crap. She would need to fly back earlier than she had planned. She logged into United's website and changed her flight. The only option was ten a.m. They would barely be able to have breakfast. Alex responded to her boss. Obviously, she would make the appointment. She almost wanted to return to the airport right now. But she did want to talk to her dad. It was odd that Cane had spoken with him and had somewhat of a heart to heart. Her chest tightened. A conversation with her father that didn't revolve around football would be nice for a change.

Her phone buzzed inside her purse.

"Are you there?"

"Surrounded by lots of maroon. Red River Rivalry paraphernalia you want me to take pics?" Alex laughed. He definitely wouldn't want pics. All four years he was the quarterback of UT they

lost to OU.

"I guess you could have gotten there sooner if Oklahoma didn't suck. Pics of you yes. RRR hell no."

A smile formed on her lips. *"Oh wow, my dad just read your text over my shoulder...I guess your lunch dates have been suspended."*

Alex left her phone on her bed. Enjoy that Rookie. She went in search of her dad. It was time for a chat. She had lied to Cane about him being sick. It was Alex who was sick. Homesick. She needed and wanted some quality time with her dad.

The house was huge. She could get in serious cardio if she looped the entire thing. Alex never understood why they had such an enormous house when it was only the two of them. But it was what it was. Being the coach of OU meant a large salary. Her dad was one of the best coaches in the nation.

He was at his desk. Did he ever rest? Alex knocked on the office door. The room was painted a maroon color and his leather chairs matched. "Hey, want to grab something to eat?"

"There is some food in the fridge." He didn't glance up at her.

"I was thinking maybe we could go out? What about Ray's?" Alex's chest tightened.

Her dad put his pen down and eyed her. "Yea, brisket sounds good."

Alex's mouth curved up into a smile. "Ha, I know your weakness."

His brow furrowed. "No weakness. But I do have questions about yours."

"Mine?"

"Yes, you write scathing articles about Cane Clayburn and the man is inviting me to lunch? Is this a ploy on his part? What's going on with the two of you?" He got up from his desk.

Alex eyed the floor. She had never had a guy chat with her dad. No one had ever met him other than at the stadium.

Her dad was hands off and had a hands-off-his-daughter motto.

"Nothing."

"Nothing? A man does not fly to have lunch with a father for nothing. Obviously, he is into you. Which I care about only if you are into him." His head cocked to the side.

Alex shook her head. "I'm into my career right now. I have an important meeting with the network at three tomorrow so I have to leave earlier than I had planned."

Her dad nodded his head and ran his finger over his jaw. It was clean shaven. He never had a five o'clock shadow. Ever. "That's great, Alexandra. I'm proud of you."

But was he or was he proud of Cane's connection with Max? Her dad was a fan of Max Argyle just as much as she was.

***

"Good morning soon-to-be-fiancé."

Alex scanned the message. He was so ridiculous. At some point she wondered if she responded with full-fledged adoration would he retreat. Maybe she would try that. No. Alex had too much self-respect to consider that further. Her stomach clenched. She did. She did have self-respect. It wasn't like she forgot. She hadn't but maybe she could let it go? Second chances and all that good stuff. No. Alex shook her head and sent a toilet emoji back to him to let him know they both knew he was talking shit.

"Wow, we've moved to the step in our relationship where you feel comfortable going to the bathroom in front of me. Nice."

Arg. No. She would never go to the bathroom in front of him. If she were with Cane, she would hit him. No. If he was in the room right now, Alex would utilize his body in other ways. So many other ways.

Her phone vibrated again. *"Or are you thinking about me and you in the bathroom together at Perry's and pleasuring yourself?"*

Of course, he would take it there. Well, she would too

and Alex wanted to, badly. *"Is that what you're doing, Corn Fed?"*

"Is that your subtle way of asking for a dick pic?"

Alex's mouth dropped open. No, she wasn't but—another text message popped up. A photograph of the most exquisite cock she had ever laid her eyes upon. It was hard and she wanted it in her mouth or thrust deep between her thighs. Her downtown area tingled. Fuck. If only they were in the same town at this moment. No doubt he would drive over and make her cum. Alex dropped her hand down to the apex of her thighs. Even without a finger inside her she knew she was wet. Cane made her wetter than she had ever been and he wasn't even in the room. But his photograph was. On her phone. In her hand. She glanced at it and ran her fingers over her clit. Softly, at first. It was important to begin with a light touch. If she or anyone else started with too much pressure it threw her entire orgasm off. It was almost like foreplay in itself. It had to be soft and slow. Work up to the more intense circles. Apply pressure with skill. There was a method to it. Alex didn't have five orgasms daily because she was Rookie of the Year. No, she was the MVP of orgasms. Sometimes at work if she was not motivated to complete an article she would retreat to the ladies and give herself an orgasm. It was no surprise that the increased serotonin levels in her brain created better articles. Words strung together in a rhythmic motion after she had reached the perfect O. Alex stroked her clit. She didn't travel with her vibrator but it wouldn't matter. There was something so pure and organic about an orgasm that was achieved via her fingers versus an electronic device.

Cane's cock was so big. Alex eyed the photo in her hand. If only he were here. Her heart skipped a beat and her chest tightened. Dayum. The vein on the side of his erection was almost as big as some actual erections she had seen. Her mouth opened. His cock tasted great. She loved the way it slipped down her throat. When she returned to Houston, she would finish the blow job she had started with him. Alex wanted to swallow his cum. It would be creamy and the right amount of salty goodness. She was a hundred percent on this. Alex's fingers increased in speed and the trickle began down her arms and thighs. Pulses of pleasure circulated through her veins. Cane. Cane. Cane. All the way. Faster. Harder. She increased her twists. Her turns. Her fingers rubbed along her clit until her veins delivered the most intense orgasm. Alex breathed a *yes*. Dayum and he wasn't even here.

***

Navy blazer. Check. Red blouse. Check. Navy skirt. On. Alex was ready for the meeting. She made her way into the studio office and let go of all her insecure thoughts. She was going to tackle this interview like the MVP of the Super Bowl. Yes. This was it. Her big game. If Alex handled this interview like her spot with Max it was a done deal. This is what Mason had said on the phone. She passed through the glass double doors and was met by a woman and man. They both clapped with enthusiasm and their giant smiles displaying shiny bright teeth.

"Alex...or do you prefer Alexandra? Jeff, what do you think, Alex or Alexandra? Which one is more trend worthy?" The woman turned her head and focused on the man who wore a plaid shirt and bow tie.

He pursed his lips and nodded. "Alexandra? Hmm...no. Alex. Yes. Alex. That works." Jeff threw up his palms and the blond woman double high fived him.

"Yesss. Alex. It is so Alex. Oh...My...Freaking...Gawd. How could it be anything other than Alex?"

Alex smiled. This couldn't be anymore awkward. She blinked to take in the scene. This was nothing like she had imagined. It was almost as if she were behind one of those mirrors that was really a glass window. The reality of her life as it played out before her; and she was not the main character.

The blond inspected her body. "Oh, fawk. Shiat. This is not good." She shook her head.

"No. Defs, not good." Jeff shook his head in the same repetition as the woman.

"No. No. No. Honey, let's circle up." The blond waved both of her hands to Jeff and Alex.

Alex stepped closer as if they had decided to break the fourth wall and include her in the performance.

"So…here's the deal. You've got to drop some serious LBs if you want to be on the small screen." The blond cocked her head to the right and nodded.

"True story." Jeff rocked his head back and forth.

Alex's insides crumbled. Lose weight? Her stomach clenched tight. The idea of her weight being an issue again was next level CPTSD. Why was she to continue on with this repeat of push and pull of possibilities of a success in her career only to be dashed because of one too many pieces of cheesecake? She hadn't realized this part of the show was going to attack her on a level she thought she had buried a long time ago. She was a size six. Yes, maybe a curvy size six. But was that not good enough?

Hopes of happiness sank beneath her skin. She took in a deep breath as she contemplated the delivery of nostalgic bad news in the studio office. She pressed her fingertips together. As if she could shrink the dagger to her dreams. Lose weight? She was too fat for television? Alex swallowed. Her eyes filled with tears. Blink. Not again. She was a size six on a good day. How was this not okay? Back in college, yes, she had been overweight. Not the typical freshman fifteen, Alex had packed on freshman fifteen times four. It had taken her two years to lose those pounds. But she did it. Because of him. It had hurt too much to eat. She no longer sought out the comfort of food. It wasn't until she lost all of it that she began to enjoy the taste of food again. Celery was her go to snack. Plain. Alex could go through an entire stalk in a day. He still had no idea. It was obvious. But she did look drastically different. That amount of weight loss does wonders for one's appearance and self-esteem. Yet in an instant, she had been gob-smacked back to college. Too fat. Too many pounds. Too hard to lift. Too damn fat. Again. Alex pressed her lips together. She would do whatever it took. She wanted this job and nothing would stand in her way.

"Okay." Alex nodded.

"Yesss, honey. Okay is right. Right now, you are a butter, ya know?" The blonde shook her head causing her hair to swing around her chiseled jaw.

"Butter?" Alex's eyebrows raised.

"Yaaah, a butter. But her. Like people like your articles etc. but your face and—" She waved her hand over her body and poked her stomach. "And body...too much." She tossed her hair. "Lose at least fifteen and you will drop the butter." She winked.

"Totes agreed." Jeff double high fived the blond. "Now, rush off to the gym and burn dem calories, yo. Tomorrow you are scheduled for sideline interviews."

"Okay, will do." Alex nodded and shook their hands. Too fat. Fine. She would lose the weight. No more ice cream. She wanted to be on-air. This was her dream. If it meant no more sweets and treats of the mouth then so be it. Well, there was one treat she could have that wouldn't be too many calories. Cane's cock. She needed it right now. Deep in her mouth where she could swallow his cum. If the calories were too much, she would work it off on him. It was time for some sexercise.

Call or text? She wanted to hear his voice but there was a piece of her that feared the idea of his voicemail. Text.

"Pre-game scrimmage?"

A lump formed in the back of her throat. Was that a stupid text? No, it was fine. He would like it. Or maybe not. Either way, his cock could clear the lump. She was sure of it.

"Home team advantage?"

A smile formed on Alex's lips. The lips that would soon

encircle his hard erection. *"My place. Twenty minutes or I'll have to sub you."*

"I can't be subbed. Ever. Be naked when I get there."

No problem. She made it home in record time and left the door unlocked. Alex was going to let him find her in bed. Maybe she would begin without him. She laughed internally.

Alex stripped off her clothes and tossed them on the chair in her room.

She climbed on her bed and ran her finger over her clit. Her phone was in her hand. She pulled up the image of Cane's cock. The apex of her thighs tingled. With an ounce of courage, she snapped a photo of her thighs and sent it to Cane.

"You're missing the kickoff."

The snap of the latch to her apartment sounded and sent a vibration deep inside of her. A tiny sense of fear that it wouldn't be Cane popped up in her mind but was quickly dismissed as his large frame crossed the threshold of her bedroom doorway.

"I can't miss kickoff if I'm already on the field." He flashed her a wide grin. His muscles flexed through his t-shirt.

"You're late, Corn Fed."

"I'm here now, that's all that matters." He threw his shirt over his head and onto the ground as he sifted his legs out of his jeans.

"I'll answer that after we review your performance."

"Great, after our seven minutes of cuddling." His lips ran along her neck. "I like that you ran with my call on no clothes."

"I was going to be naked with or without you, Corn Fed." She reached down and stroked his cock.

"It would still be with me because you would be thinking about me. Tell me how many times you've looked at my photo." Cane rubbed his erection against her clit.

"None."

"What did I tell you about lying, sweetheart?" He circled his cock over her point of pleasure.

"Quit teasing me."

"Tell me how many times." He thrust the tip of his erection in between her legs.

Alex bucked her hips in an attempt to take Cane in. He pulled back. Alex's hand grasped his cock. "Come on, the clock is ticking."

"You know I like overtime." His mouth met hers and their tongues twisted together. This was what she needed. A distraction. Her mind was swept away into a point of ecstasy and he thrust deep inside of her. Finally.

"I knew you wouldn't hold out forever. Corn Fed, you put yourself in the danger zone. You were about to get traded out." She wrapped her legs around his hips as he slammed into her harder.

"No subs." He pushed deeper. "No extra players." He was so deep she couldn't speak. "Just us." He lowered his mouth to her breasts. First, he sucked on her nipples, then he kissed each one with such intensity it threw Alex over the edge, slamming her into a crescendo of euphoria. A sensation akin to a million pieces of shattered glaciers splintered across her skin. Light made up of white and gold scattered in front of her eyes. Dayum. He rolled over and pulled her body into his. She let out a deep breath. Her heart raced in her chest. Cane patted her butt.

"Such a great ass. Plenty to hold on to. Nobody would fumble with this."

Alex recoiled. Arg. She needed to get to the gym. "Ha, which is why I need to run. You've got to go." She hopped up out of bed.

"We just worked out. Now we cuddle remember?" He pulled her back down to the bed and wrapped his arms around her.

"No, I can't. I really have to run. You realize TV adds extra weight, which might be fine for a quarterback but not a reporter." She wrestled out of his arms and made her way to the bathroom.

Alex threw on her workout clothes and found Cane in her living room. Cane raised his eyebrows. "Gym clothes and ice cream works for me." He flashed her a white toothed grin.

She shook her head. "Just when I was beginning to think you had some brains up there, I have to use pictures to explain it to you. I'm going to run. No ice cream." Alex grabbed a pen and paper and drew an ice cream cone then marked it with an x. She handed him the paper.

Cane laughed. "Fine, replay at my house tonight?"

"Hello, I am on-air tomorrow. If I were to stay at your house you would keep me up all night. No away games." She opened her door and he followed her out into the hallway.

"Alright, sweetheart. I'll make reservations for Masraff's." He pulled her in close and kissed her hard like it would be a year until the next time their lips would meet.

"No way. I have zero self-control and cannot walk in through those doors without eating the Chocolate Mouse Napolean." She licked her lips. The berry infused whipped cream would be so much fun to lick off of Cane. No. No more desserts.

"I'll pick you up at seven." He tugged on her pony tail.

Alex laughed. "Not happening. Besides, I don't ride with guys in cars unless the relationship is going somewhere."

"That's funny. You don't need an escape plan with me."

She did though. Alex couldn't go all in with him, not again. "It's not a joke." It was true. Alex always had an out and that meant being behind the wheel of her own car.

"You're a great writer but your stand up needs some work." Cane slapped her on the behind.

Alex rolled her eyes and sighed. "I'll see you on the sidelines."

"I'll see you for dinner."

***

Alex regained her composure as the image of Cane faded in her rearview mirror. Too much. She shouldn't have called him. It was like they were boyfriend and girlfriend and she couldn't do that. Not with him. Being official with Cane would only mean heartbreak, she was sure of it. No. That would have to be it. Her chest tightened. Air escaped from her lungs. No, she couldn't *not* see him. They would see each other. But not date. Alex let out a deep sigh. It was not meant to be. He had called the play in the huddle and changed it at the line. She couldn't go through that again. Alex knew who the mike was in this relationship. Being tackled again was one replay at the down she didn't want to repeat. Honesty was the only way to resolve this situation and the pain that burned against her chest. It was time to snap the ball.

CHAPTER THIRTEEN

Cane's eyes narrowed when Alex opened the door. She was wearing his jersey and nothing else. Her hair was wet like she had just got out of the shower. "I wasn't expecting round two until after dinner, but I'm always game." Cane pulled her against his chest and kissed her hard.

After a few minutes, Alex pulled back. "What are you doing here?"

"I told you we have dinner plans."

Alex lifted the celery stalk she was eating. "I can't. I told you that. We had an entire conversation about it less than two hours ago. You've taken one too many blows to the head, Corn Fed if you can't remember that."

"I remember you making some bullshit excuse but we're still going to dinner."

A furrow formed between her brows. She was sexy when she was annoyed. Lucky for him, he annoyed her a lot. "I can't go to dinner at Massraf's. I have no will power when it comes to that place. I was serious when I said I needed to diet. I am going to be on camera now. Time to shake this writer's ass." As if to demonstrate she lifted the hem of the jersey.

"Dang, woman. Looks good to me." Cane grabbed a

cheek and squeezed. "Feels even better. Want me to show you how much I like it?"

Alex pulled the shirt down. "Camera ready," she repeated, waving the stalk of celery. "I'm serious."

"And I'm serious that I love that ass. Don't get rid of it. We're friends. I am *really* fond of that ass. I will miss it, like go into serious mourning if it leaves and then we won't make the playoffs. Texans will lose all because of you. Don't do that to the fans, sweetheart."

Alex laughed. "I'm glad you have a special bond with my backside but the rest of America doesn't share your affection."

"Only because they haven't seen it. Here, let me show them." Cane pulled out his phone. "Show me that ass, sweetheart."

"No! You're ridiculous."

"I really am but now I want a picture of your ass. Don't worry, I'm not going to show anyone. This one is all for me. Want me to send you the picture of what I do when I look at it?"

Alex flushed. "You already sent me one," she reminded him.

"There is a fresh one every day. You provide me with a lot of material to work with. Come on, show me your ass. It's only fair. I did a strip tease for you."

Alex laughed and shook her head. "One picture. And if I find it on any big bottomed fetish sites, I will ghost you for good."

Cane laughed. "As if I would do that. This ass belongs on my-girlfriend-has-a-perfect-ass fetish site." He clicked the camera icon and admired the photos. "Will be using these for years when I am playing in other cities and I can't see my woman."

Alex rolled her eyes and bit into her celery.

"Woman stop eating the celery, I am taking you to dinner. I don't take you out enough. Seriously, put the stalk down. You're going to ruin your appetite."

Alex stared at him dubiously. "I really won't."

Unease settled in him. She really thought she needed to lose weight. "Don't diet to fit some mold, Alex. You're beautiful but that's not why you got this job. You got this job because you are a good journalist."

She shrugged her shoulders. "This is part of my job. You should understand that. You lift heavy things for like four hours a day because it is part of your job."

Cane shook his head. Alex tried to look away but he forced her head back round to face him. "I lift weights to perform well in my job. The size of your ass will not affect your performance. You're a good journalist. And you're sexy. But those two things have nothing to do with each other." Did she really not get that?

"Look, I don't want to go to dinner." Alex pulled away and he didn't try to stop her. That's what she did when she was upset, she retreated into herself. He could argue the point until he was hoarse and she wouldn't hear a single word because she had already shut the conversation down.

Cane pulled her back. "Alex, I will support you in this because I will support you on everything. But I don't agree. Your body is perfect. No, don't look away. I need you to hear that."

Alex was quiet for a long moment. She stared down at the hands that held her against him. She bit her lip as she considered what he said. "What if I wasn't perfect? What if I gained weight? Lots of weight...say sixty pounds."

Cane had to smile. It was an oddly specific number. He leaned down and kissed her forehead.

"You will probably gain that much when you're pregnant and it won't put me off. Is that what you're hoping for? To get a break from me? Cause that ain't going to happen. Even if we have to widen the doors and reinforce the furniture, I will still want you. I love your body, because it is *your* body."

Alex stared up at him with dark eyes, clearly unconvinced, but she didn't say anything. She wouldn't. She hated to argue. She ran from conflict. Cane let go of her and lifted up his shirt. He pointed at the grooved plane of his abs. "I have no doubt this twelve pack will go when I retire. I might even lose my hair. Will you still want me?"

"Of course. I mean, I will miss the twelve pack but I will have plenty of pictures of it by then to get me by. And there is always your Twitter feed."

"So, you will still be into me, but I am shallower than that. As soon as your body changes, I'm out? Is that it?"

Alex stared him straight in the eye. "Yes."

She didn't pull away this time, no retreating from conflict. The honesty of her answer surprised him. When did he ever give her the impression that what they had was dependent upon the way she looked? He hadn't even found her beautiful when they first got together, because he was an idiot. But now she was the most beautiful woman he had ever met. He couldn't tell her that though, it would hardly help his case.

"Why?" he asked. "Why do you expect me to be shallow?"

Alex blinked like she wasn't expecting the question. "Because men are visual people."

Cane ran a hand through his cropped hair. "I'm going to ignore that blatant sexism, Alex. I expect more from you."

Alex bit her lip again, hard enough to make it bleed, the skin drained of color where the incisors pressed. Eventually she spoke. "That's the point, Cane. I don't expect more from you. We're doing this now because it suits you. But what about when it doesn't?"

"Why would I stop wanting you?" he asked incredulously. Annoyance grew within him. Why did she still think this was some flash in the pan thing? How had he ever given her the impression that he was not all in?

She shook her head. "Because the saying about history repeating itself is often true."

She looked so sad and defeated. He was torn between wanting to gather her in his arms and comfort her, or shaking her to knock some sense into her. Under his annoyance, disappointment spread. What they had didn't mean a whole hell of a lot if she didn't trust him.

"What history? Is it all men you think so poorly of or just me?" He wasn't sure he wanted to know the answer but he asked anyway. He needed to know.

Alex was quiet for too long. He had pushed her too far and she had retreated. Eventually she said, "You for sure. I don't know about other men yet. I hope I can find someone I trust. I want to."

Her words were like a blow to the chest. Unbelievable. After everything, she didn't trust him. What was he supposed to do? Agitation clawed at him. "You don't trust me? I am the one pushing for more." Could she hear herself? She was the one shutting them down at every pass. She was the one who refused to acknowledge they were in a relationship. She was the one who kept dating other people after they started dating. And yet, he was the one who shouldn't be trusted. Cane rubbed at his temples. He had a headache and he needed to eat dinner. Unlike Alex, he was still a fan of three-square meals a day. "I am too hungry for this conversation. What do you have?"

Cane didn't wait for Alex to answer. He was too annoyed with her on an empty stomach. "You have no food in your kitchen." Cane shut the refrigerator and opened her cupboards.

"I have eggs and celery. Oh, and coffee," Alex offered. "I need to go shopping." Her excuse was pathetic. She was lying and they both knew it.

Cane was starting to get pissed. Was she not eating now to lose weight? He needed to shut that down hard. "I am ordering pizza. I need to eat if I am going to win this argument." He pulled out his phone and dialed Papa John's. He wasn't a huge fan of pizza but he had an endorsement deal with them. The commercial he did for them paid for his house, so it only seemed right he order from them. Plus, he knew for a fact Alex was a fan of pizza. He ordered a large combination pizza to be delivered.

"Now, where were we?" Cane sat beside Alex on her couch. She did not look up when he sat down, she just stared at her hands.

"I had a date tonight." Her voice was so soft he barely heard her.

The anger he felt before took hold and grew arms and legs. "What?" he demanded. She didn't trust *him* yet she'd had a date. Unfuckingbelievable. Still, she would not look at him. Frustration mounted in him. He could not do this one sided.

"I canceled. On the way to the gym, I had this 'what are you doing moment'. I had to cancel. Dating some other guy wouldn't be fair to him, or me, or you. I don't want to date anyone else. I don't want to go to dinner with anyone else or have sex with anyone else or go skinny dipping with anyone else." Finally, she turned to him. She looked so sad. Why? Why was she sad? He wanted to kiss her until she smiled again. But he couldn't, not now, not until he knew what was wrong and how he could fix it. "But I don't want to date you, either. I am trying to keep this causal but one day I will wake up and realize I am in love with you and then when you back away I will be devastated. I can't do that. Not again." Alex looked away again. She didn't want to tell him this. Any of it. He could tell. She didn't do emotions.

"Again?"

Alex looked back at him. Her eyes narrowed in question.

"You said again." Cane reached for her hand. "Who broke your heart? Who?" He realized after he asked that he didn't want to know. They both had a past but that didn't matter. Anything that happened before they met, was just that, in the past. "Whoever he was, he was an asshole. You're better off without him."

Alex laughed but there was no merriment, it was a bitter sound. She shook her head. "You really have no idea, do you? You don't get it."

She tried to pull her hands away again but Cane would not let her. "I get it. I get that the only thing that can stop us is you. I'm in. Both feet, sweetheart. Let's do it. You and me, let's do this. No more joking, no more pulling back. All in." Alex swallowed. She opened her mouth to speak and he knew it would be another excuse. He had heard enough. It was time to get real and stop playing games. "Look, this is new to me. You know that. I put my cards on the table right from the start. I have never had a serious relationship until you. And some asshole has hurt you so we're both rookies. But if anyone can make it work it is us. Don't let fear stop you. Please don't be a coward about this."

Her jaw set in determination like he hoped it would. This was her weakness, her need to prove herself, and he was using it against her. And he didn't even feel a little bit bad about it. There were very few things he wouldn't do to win her. "Yeah, you were hurt," he continued. "You were sacked hard. But you get back up and shake it off. Trust me, getting taken down is part of my job."

She shook her head but there was a slight smile pulling up her full lips. "It really shouldn't be part of your job. If your blindside was covered—"

Cane grabbed her and pulled her in against him. "Right there is why I will never get tired of you. You are smart and beautiful and you know as much about football as any player in the league. I must remember to thank your dad for that the next time I take him to lunch."

Alex pulled back. "No. No more lunch dates with my dad."

"He's my girlfriend's dad, so lunch is going to happen. And I will send him tickets and I will invite him to charity golf tournaments. Deal with it."

Alex made an exasperated sound. "Not girlfriend. I really don't like the sound of that." She paused for a second to consider. "We're free agents. Okay, just trying for a spot on the team. We will see how it goes."

Cane had to force himself not to smile. What Alex was proposing was every bit the relationship he wanted but her semantics were different. She used a football analogy because that was her comfort zone. Lucky for him, he too was fluent in football. "I can already tell you that you have a spot on my team." He kissed her then pulled back to whisper against her lips. "And remember free agents can only play without a contract in the pre-season then they need to sign." He was pushing her, but she needed to be pushed.

"Let's see if we're good enough to make the team before we start contract negotiations." She leaned in and kissed him, her mouth opening for him. Suddenly she pulled back, her eyes wide.

"Nobody can know about this. I'm serious. It is totally unprofessional. I am a reporter. I can't be…" Alex struggled to find the right word.

"Girlfriend. You're my girlfriend. Nobody can know you're my girlfriend," he offered for her.

"Yes. That. No one can know that. I mean, my dad knows because you had to go and see him," she said clearly chagrined. "But no one else. I haven't even told my best friend, Vanessa. This is top secret. Okay?"

Cane smiled. "Naughty. I love it. You're getting hotter by the minute. How could I ever get tired of you? It's our little secret. I mean we will tell our kids, right, so they know they're not bastards."

Alex shook her head. "If you start talking about your eleven-pound babies that you're going to have with your brood mare wife, I will show you the door, Corn Fed. We are trialing this…thing."

"This thing," he repeated. "We should probably consummate this thing. Let's make it official."

"You're ridiculous. Sex on my couch won't make it any more official." She rolled her eyes.

"No, but it is fun."

Alex pushed him off her. "Your pizza will be here any minute."

Cane kissed her neck as his hand reached under the jersey. "I can be quick."

The doorbell rang. With a groan Cane stood up. He opened the door. The pizza delivery boy let out a squawking sound like he was in pain then dropped the pizza box. The kid, who looked like he was barely old enough to drive didn't move. He was frozen in place, transfixed.

"You alright?" Cane bent down to pick up the box. He handed the kid fifty dollars. "Keep the change."

The kid opened his mouth to speak a few times before anything came out. "You're…you're…you're Cane Clayburn."

Cane smiled. "Yeah, I am. Pleasure to meet you, Josh." He read the kid's name tag. Cane reached his hand out to shake. He didn't ask the kid if he was a Texans fan because it seemed obvious. Cowboys' fans reacted by telling him every wrong play he had ever called. He far preferred the reaction of Texan fans.

"Nobody is going to believe it. You eat Papa John's. We were actually talking about this tonight at work. I wonder if Cane Clayburn really eats Papa Johns."

"I hope you put money on it. Cause I do."

"Nah, I wish I had now. Seriously no one is going to believe it. You're Cane Clayburn. How cool is that."

Alex came up behind him and took the box. "It's pretty cool," she said. There was glee in her voice. She sat the box down on the coffee table. "Do you have a phone? I will take your picture together," Alex offered.

Josh nodded like a bobble-head doll on the dashboard of a car. Alex took the phone and snapped several pictures before she handed the phone back.

"This is so cool," Josh repeated over and over.

"Totally cool," Alex agreed. "Have a good night." Alex smiled as she shut the door. "Your legion of fans."

"You're the only fan I care about."

Alex stood on her tiptoes and kissed his cheek. "You have your pizza. I am going to have some quality time with the Salvatore brothers."

"I know who they are now, by the way. I Googled it. Did

not peg you as a vampire fan."

"You googled The Vampire Diaries?"

"Of course. I had to know who this Salvatore punk was that was making my girl hot."

Alex laughed. "Eat your pizza, Corn Fed."

CHAPTER FOURTEEN

Alex sat down on the couch. The pizza smelled amazing but not as amazing as her new job. The Salvatore brothers would offer some distraction until Cane was finished. Her phone vibrated on the table. It scooted across the surface with every ring. She recognized her best friend's number.

"Hey Vanessa, what's up?"

"What's up? You tell me. You're dating Cane fricken Clayburn and you didn't tell me. When did that happen?" Vanessa demanded.

Alex glanced over at Cane, and prayed Vanessa wasn't loud enough to be overheard. Alex slid off the couch and took the call in her bedroom. "It's complicated. And we're not telling anyone." Guilt stabbed at Alex's chest. They had been best friends since college. Vanessa knew her better than anyone. She knew exactly why things would never work out with Cane. Alex should have told her. She thought about it after the first night. To call and pour her heart out but that wasn't Alex's style. And she didn't need to give her best friend the opportunity to tell her how incredibly stupid she was. She already knew that. Cane made her stupid. When she was around him, she forgot. All the hurt disappeared. Ahh, she was crazy. This was such a bad idea.

Vanessa laughed. "That's cute, Alex. But there is no secret, the entire world knows."

"What? What are you talking about? I haven't told anyone. I promise. I would never tell anyone before I told you." Alex pulled on the ends of her hair.

"That's sweet, but you don't need to worry about telling anyone. Everyone knows now."

A sinking sensation pulled down sharply on the pit of her stomach. Vanessa didn't even have to explain. She already knew...the pizza delivery guy.

How stupid was she? *Here let me take your picture.* Stupid. Stupid. Stupid. And she was wearing his jersey with nothing else. His god damn name was written across her back. Oh shit. Her chest tightened. She concentrated on filling her lungs with air but her body would not cooperate. This was not okay and it was certainly not professional. This wasn't the message she wanted to be sending to the network. *Hire me on a full-time basis. I sleep with players. Oh, God.* "Okay, I have to handle this. I'll call you back tomorrow."

"It is what it is. It's your business and now the business of every American with the internet. Laters."

Alex shook her head and cut the call. She could always count on Vanessa to keep it real. There was no pretending with her. Alex took a deep breath to brace herself before she typed in Cane's name. Instantly it returned with stories of him sleeping with a reporter. *A reporter,* wasn't horrible. There were lots of sports reporters...not many women but still enough to muddy the water. She continued to scroll until she saw it. Her name. She was named publicly as the reporter sleeping with Cane. Okay, she could handle this. She logged onto her socials. Oh shit. All but one hashtag was about Cane or her and Cane. Number one was #CaneSacksAlex, number two was #CaneBedsAlex. Her entire feed was full of hashtags about Cane. #CanePlaysAlex   #CaneTDSAlex   #CaneMVPSAlex #AlexRookieOfTheYearCane #AlexBedsCane #ABC. Bile rose in the back of her mouth. Not okay.

This was really not okay. She turned off her phone and closed her eyes so she could pretend she had not just seen the demise of her career, but the words were burned into her head. Even when she closed her eyes, they were there. She let out a stream of air. Regroup. Focus. Plan. Suddenly strong arms were wrapped tightly around her.

"Breathe," Cane whispered.

She tried. Did he know? Had he seen it too? What was she thinking, of course he did, and that is why he had her in his arms. He wanted to comfort her. It was obvious. It didn't matter, in this moment she didn't care. As soon as he let her go, realization would flood her, but right now this was good. His arms around her. It was what she needed.

"How did you find out?" she whispered.

"Coach called me."

Alex's heart sank. This was real. Everyone knew. "I'm sorry," she murmured.

Cane pulled back. He tilted her chin until their eyes met. "Don't be sorry. I'm not sorry. I have a sexy girlfriend and the world knows about it. I'm good."

Alex squeezed her eyes shut. "All my credibility has been dumped into an ocean of missed opportunities."

"Look at me, Alex."

She forced herself to open her eyes.

"I am not ashamed of us. You should not be ashamed of us. No one will ever accuse you of favoritism. You do remember the articles you have written about me, right? You're definitely not doing me any favors because I am the best lover you have ever had."

Alex smiled despite herself. "True."

"True, that I'm your best lover. I'm going to need that in writing."

"Yes, that too, but true that I have not shown you any favoritism."

"Yeah, the opposite of that, actually. So, we can play this two ways. Admit it and let the story burn itself out, or shut it down hard. I haven't told anyone. I doubt you have told anyone. There are no pictures of us together. Just the word of a pimply teenage boy. All I need to say is that the woman wasn't you. It's up to you, Alex."

Alex nodded. He was right. She wasn't in any of the photos. They could just deny it. That is what they would do—act like it didn't happen. They would be more careful. She needed to remember that people recognized her since the Max Argyle interview. The piece had been picked up nationally. She was recognizable now in the small circle of sports fans. She would not make that mistake again. "Yes, let's deny it." She pressed her lips together.

Cane's smile faltered, tightened even but he nodded. "If that's what you want."

"Yes, that's what I want. No one can know about us. Ever."

"Fine." His deep voice was curt. He sighed as he turned and went back to the kitchen.

CHAPTER FIFTEEN

This was not good. Last two seconds on the clock and the Texans were going to lose to the Patriots. It was their first away game and the score was twenty-one to nineteen. Even with a safety that would only tie things and Patriots had the ball. Cane paced the sideline. In less than a minute Alex would have to interview him. She would have to face him in a time of failure and ask him how he felt about it. Her stomach growled. Not only was it completely empty, but now bile sloshed around inside of it. This was not a moment of pleasure for her. Alex wanted to be an on-air reporter but this…this sideline interview was going to be bad. She pressed her lips together.

"Ready?" Alistair held his camera over his head. He towered over her and Alex was wearing three-inch leather boots.

"Yes, how are my teeth?" Alex flashed him an open mouth smile.

"No lipstick, you're good." He nodded and gave her a thumbs up.

"Okay Fonzi, let's do this."

The whistle sounded and the players rushed off the field. Alex patted down her hair. It was cold. She had forgone the hat and scarf as she didn't need to add extra layers to her body. Her suede skirt barely withheld the cold from her legs and the red cashmere sweater that covered her arms was a sad layer of fabric that had failed to keep her warm.

Cane rushed over to her side. His eyes were an ice blue. They appeared lighter. Almost a reflection of the cold air and the atmosphere of the loss.

"Alex Martin here with Cane Clayburn, it's the first away game of the season for the Texans and it's a loss. How are you feeling right now?"

Cane nodded his head and ran his thumb over his jaw. "I'm disappointed. Sometimes the calls don't go your way and that's always disappointing."

"You think the incomplete in the second quarter wasn't right?'

Cane raised a brow at her. "Austin looked inside the line to me but the sideline ref would have a better viewpoint. So that is just one of those things that once it's been called you have to move on to the next play."

"You were sacked six times tonight. Almost tied the record. When are they going to sub in a different left tackle?" Alex's chest tightened. The coach for the Texans put Cane in danger for a re-injury to his shoulder along with every other body part. Alex wanted zero of Cane's parts being hurt. The left tackle needed to be subbed. He was not doing his job. Time for him to go.

He bit his lip. "That's a coach call. We are all out there together as a team. If I go down, we all go down."

"If your blindside was protected you wouldn't have gone down," Alex pressed further. Maybe she shouldn't, but she had to.

"There are eleven players on the field once the ball is snapped, with a million different possibilities of how the play will run. Football is literally a live chess match with more bruises." He nodded. She would bring this up later. A live chess match. It might be time for them to play. Alex could really get off on the idea of Cane being in check.

The sacks he took had to have left some serious bruises on his body. "How is your shoulder feeling?"

"Great, thank you." Cane moved past her. That was a lie. She was sure of it.

Alex scanned the field. She needed to chat with Marquez, the man had been on fire tonight. His touchdown antics were even hotter. He did a full-on dance routine in the end zone that was better than the halftime show, and he had done it three times tonight.

"Marquez, congratulations on a great game. Any part of the game that was a highlight for you?" Alex turned the mic toward his mouth. The crowd was loud. Patriot's fans really enjoyed their beer and this was a moment to pour even more. Hops filled the stadium.

Marquez licked his lips. "Hey Alex, it's good to see you with a mic. You looked really good on that interview with Max."

"Thank you. What was your favorite moment in tonight's game?" Alex nodded to encourage him to answer the question. This was an interview not a speed date session.

"Man, I don't know. There were so many great ones. I just love a solid touchdown. You know what I mean?" He licked his lips. "So, since you're not dating Clayburn how about I take you to the end zone?" Marquez scooped her up in his arms and charged down to the end zone.

"Marquez put me down." Alex pushed against his body.

He laughed and continued to run.

"I'm serious put me down." She wriggled out of his grip. Alex stood tall and tugged her skirt down. She was mortified. That was completely inappropriate. As Cane crossed the corner of her vision, he charged toward them and tackled Marquez. He laid on top of Marquez and pummeled him.

"Don't ever lay a hand on her again." Cane gripped his jersey as he silenced him with his eyes.

"Hey man, she's a free agent, right?"

"No, she's not." He slammed him down on the ground

as two refs pulled him back. Every single camera in the stadium was on Cane and Alex. Live footage.

Oh. My. God.

Great. Her first live on-air performance and it was something out of an episode of Friday Night Lights. Alex didn't need or want this immaturity. She wasn't in high school. She was a professional and this scene was the complete opposite of that. Alex made her way out of the stadium, her heart pounding against her chest. The studio had seen enough of her sideline performance. It was time to get out of here. The crowd couldn't be louder but all Alex could hear was *"No, she's not."* On repeat.

But she wasn't anymore. She was done with this game. No more. It had to end tonight. No. She didn't want it to end. Shit. Even though she knew the road they were on, she didn't want to get off. Why? Why did he have this effect on her? Why couldn't she be wise and stop? This would not end well. It wouldn't. Alex slid her hotel key into the door. They were supposed to get together after the game. But she wanted to cancel. The end zone tackle with Marquez was too much. But even more than that was that he said she wasn't a free agent. Like he had a say over her. No. He didn't. No.

Against her own better judgement, she glanced at Twitter. Of course they were all the #hashtags which included #NotAFreeAgent. Her phone vibrated.

"Fab sideline, but so perf with the end zone tackle, was that planned? ;)" It was Hailee from the studio. The air from Alex's lungs felt sucked out. She took in a deep breath as if she could resuscitate herself.

"Thank you. No, unscripted." She left her phone on the side chair and grabbed some celery that she had packed out of the fridge. At least she hadn't been fired, yet. The sound of knocks against her hotel door made her jump.

Cane's massive frame reflected at her through the small glass peep hole. Alex opened the door and let him in.

"How much were you fined?" Alex shut the door and

her hands found their way to her hips.

"It doesn't matter. Whatever it is it was worth every penny." He made his way to the small table in the corner, and set down several bags on it. Cane strode toward Alex. Anger fumed inside her mind. Cane ignored the obvious frown on her face as his hands pulled her toward him. He leaned down to kiss her.

Alex held up her index finger. "You can't do that again."

The sides of his mouth pulled up. "Sweetheart, no one touches my girlfriend."

"No, this is my career. You can't do that. I can handle myself." She poked his chest.

"It's my job to handle those types of situations. No punk ass is going to man handle my woman." His lips ran along her neck. "Ever." He breathed into her ear. Little bumps of pleasure spread over the back of her neck.

"We don't have a contract. I can cut you at any time." She pulled back.

Cane shook his head. "Not going to happen. But let's eat first. I'm starving." He picked through the bags and pulled out a bucket from KFC.

"Are you serious? You brought chicken in a bucket to my hotel room?" She raised an eyebrow at him.

"Ahem. Our hotel room. I'm staying the night. And I'm going to hold you all night long. Consider tonight the Super Bowl of Cuddling." He let out a laugh.

Alex couldn't help but laugh with him. "You are funny. But you are not staying the night."

Cane finished off a chicken leg and wiped his hands on a napkin. He picked up her phone and pulled up the calendar app. "See this." He tapped the screen. "Super Bowl of Cuddling. It's even on your phone, Alex. Don't act like this is a surprise." He gave her the phone.

She blinked several times. It was in her phone. How and when had he done this? Her nostrils flared. With two clicks it was deleted. "It's not there anymore." Alex raised an eyebrow.

"But I am." He scooped up some mashed potatoes. "Here try these, almost as good as the ones at Perry's."

Alex stepped back and waved her hand. "No. I'm good." She scanned through her phone. "How many dates did you schedule?"

"A lot. But I think we need to change my name in your phone. Corn Fed is fine every once in a while, but I think Soon-to-be-Fiancé has a better ring to it." He stuffed the rest of his fluffy white biscuit in his mouth.

"No. I think I will just delete your number from my phone all together." Alex held up her phone and pushed the red button so Cane could watch.

Cane laughed. "I'm not a number you can't delete me." He gathered her in his arms and pressed his lips against hers. The anger that traveled through her veins had begun to escape. She opened her mouth to him and he latched onto her tongue. With the speed of a house drenched in gasoline that had been set ablaze, Cane undressed both of them. He laid her down on the bed and kissed his way over her stomach and down her thighs until his face was on top of her clit. Cane's tongue swirled over her pleasure zone and paused. "Can a number do that?"

Alex's chest tightened. "Corn Fed, don't pause on me."

"Tell me, Alex. It's a simple yes or no answer then I'll continue."

"No." She pushed him away from her lips. Alex didn't want to, but she did want Cane to continue.

His tongue began to circle again and he lowered his face further until his tongue began to stroke deep inside of her while his thumb increased the rate of speed on her clit.

"Cane." She moaned.

He was going to send her over the edge into the oblivion of orgasmic ecstasy. Faster and faster, he inserted his tongue into her as he made a merry go round of pleasure on her clit. Her skin sizzled until the fire transferred into a snowy blast that burst through her veins and spread over her body. It reached the bottom of her feet, and her toes curled from the intensity.

Cane slammed into her. "Can a number do that?" He breathed against her neck. He was so deep he hadn't even given her a chance to catch her breath. He thrust deeper. "Alex, tell me." An array of goosebumps spread across her arms. Cane pulled out so she could fill her lungs with air. She let out a deep breath.

"What are you doing?" Alex squeezed his biceps. His muscles were so large she couldn't even curl her fingers around half of them.

"Say it, Alex." His eyes were a cool shade of blue and they matched his confidence. There was no way to deny it. He knew what he was doing at all times. Except the one time. But now was not the time for bad memories.

"Say what, Corn Fed. Come on, don't choke. Give it to me."

"I will, once you say 'Cane, you are not a number.'" He pushed his cock near the apex of her thighs.

Alex lifted her hips as if she could capture his erection and guide him back in. Cane let out a laugh. "I know what you want, Alex and you know what I want." He ran his finger along her jaw and over her lips. His finger was rough. She bit at it then began to suck on the tip.

"We can do that, too. But I know what you really want right now and that's not it." He leaned down to her ear. "Say it Alex, don't be afraid." His words were like drops of lava and they flowed into her mind and down to the organ that was afraid. He wanted her to be vulnerable. A safety. He wanted her to let down her guard of protection. Could she do it?

She released his finger from her mouth. "Cane, you are not a num—"

He rammed deep into her. The power behind his erection was like she had been sacked and he had cut off her voice. He thrust faster and harder until he reached her cervix. His cock made contact with the most ultimate of places and a tidal wave of ice and lava boiled through her skin in a repetitious tsunami of revelry. Over and over waves passed energy through her veins as he continued to pulse deep within her. It took her to the highest level possible. The crest was a mixture of white and blue until it went clear.

Like an underwater volcano the warmth of Cane's satisfaction filled Alex's insides. He slipped out of her and wrapped his arms around her. Her chest rested against his heart. The beats were a rhythm of something more than desire as it vibrated against her ear. This was different. This wasn't merely pleasure of two bodies that had sexual chemistry. It was more.

"You have no idea how hot it is when you say my name as I pound deep inside you."

"You asked me to say it."

"You said it before but I wanted to hear it again."

"No, I didn't." She shoved him.

Cane captured her hands and kissed her knuckles. "You said it right before your first orgasm."

Alex's cheeks warmed. She had no idea if she had or hadn't. Her mind was full of pleasure in that moment. Who knows what she shared.

"Alex, it's okay to be honest about your feelings. You don't exactly have a poker face."

Honest. She should be honest with him but she couldn't bring herself to do it. Besides, it wasn't entirely up to her. He played an equal part and it wasn't her fault that he had no idea. She snuggled in closer to him and inhaled his scent. Tobacco and spices with a mix of vanilla. His cologne reminded her of sexiness and something else. A sensation that she had never experienced in bed before. It was a moment of comfort and security, like when she slipped into her favorite pair of jeans. Size six. Alex had begun to lose weight and the sixes were back in action. Being a six meant so much more than the number. It was the idea of motivation and the level of success over her self-control. The security of her job now that she was able to lose the weight so she could be on air. It was everything to her and

Cane was this. He was security and he was comfort and he was something else. Something she couldn't bring herself to think. No, it was too soon. She wasn't sure if she would ever be ready again. Had Alex ever been ready before or had it been an infatuation? No, the hurt that followed wouldn't have been so strong if it had only been a crush.

CHAPTER SIXTEEN

Alex needed a push. Cane knew her well enough to know that their relationship would not progress if he didn't push it. He also knew her well enough to know timing was key. It was a delicate balance. If he pushed too hard, she would retreat but if he didn't, they would continue in secret forever, though the secret part was laughable, most people suspected even though Alex vehemently denied it.

Things were good between them, really good, but only in private and only at her house or hotels. He couldn't take her out in case they were recognized, so their relationship was confined to hotel trysts and while hotel sex was great, Cane was past booty calls. He wanted stable, normal, he would even settle for a bit of mundane. Most importantly, he wanted what his brothers had found, their person, the one who was always there for them.

Cane dialed Alex's number.

"Hey, shouldn't you be getting ready?" Alex answered without saying hello.

"I'm ready. We're about to come out for the coin toss, are you here?"

"Of course. I am the human icicle on the fifty-yard line. New York in late October is cold. Are you wearing long

143

sleeves under your jersey? You better be, Corn Fed. It's cold."

Cane smiled. That is how Alex said I love you, with worrying. He would prefer the actual words but he would take what he could get. "Hey, I forgot to ask you something," he said, ignoring her question rather than lie and tell her he was wearing long sleeves. "I don't have a game next week."

"I know. You're spending the weekend at my place. You just don't know it yet. I already have the box set of *Vampire Diaries* ready to go. You are finally going to meet the Salvatore brothers."

Cane groaned. Alex had been threatening him with *Vampire Diaries* for the better part of a month.

"Or we could spend it at mine and watch *The Usual Suspects* and eat chicken from a bucket. I'm voting for that."

"Um, no to chicken in a bucket—"

"Fine. No bucket of chicken. *Vampire Diaries* at my house on Friday after practice."

"My apartment is closer to the stadium."

Alex had still never been to his house. She always had an excuse. She was still enjoying the home field advantage but it was time for an away game. This was the next step, time to push. "My house is where we're raising our eight kids so you should probably see it so you can start picking out nursery colors. I am thinking burnt orange would be perfect for a boy or girl."

"Eight? It was seven before. You added one last month after the Patriots game which took it to seven. You can't just be arbitrarily adding kids. And progeny should not be used as punishment."

"Ooh, look at you, using that thesaurus I bought you. So sexy. My house at seven or we're having nine kids."

"You're ridiculous."

"So you keep telling me. See you Friday."

"Be careful, Cane. I mean it. I will have words with your left tackle if you get sacked at any point in the next three hours." The edge in her voice made him smile. He had no doubt she would.

"What part of keeping it on the down low would that be?"

"I'm serious. Be. Careful."

"I love you, too."

"I didn't say that." Alex laughed.

"But you feel it."

"I like to feel you." She laughed again. "I think you're getting it confused with that."

***

Five days was too long to go without seeing Alex. They had spoken everyday but she had spent the week in Connecticut filming a segment for ESPN. Thankfully she was coming home today and she would be back to reporting from the sidelines. It was bad enough to deal with all the travelling without having her permanently based in another city. Cane's heart picked up speed when the doorbell finally rang.

"You're late, sweetheart." Cane lifted Alex up and kissed her. Eventually she pulled back. "Don't try to distract me with your hot body. We're watching *The Vampire Diaries*."

Cane nodded. "We are, while we cuddle on the couch."

Alex scrunched up her nose. "No! You can't change the goal posts. There was no mention of cuddling. You're going to get a penalty here in a minute."

"Sweetheart, the cuddling was implied and you didn't veto it then. The time for negotiations has passed."

"Not impressed with you, Corn Fed. Now let me down."

"Being carried was also implied." He tried to kiss her again but she turned her head.

"Not just a penalty, you're getting fined."

"I can afford it. Now kiss me."

Alex sighed like she was trying to resist but eventually her fingers laced through his hair and she pulled his mouth to her. Her legs tangled behind his back as her bag dropped to the tiled floor. Cane kissed her as he carried her through to the kitchen and sat her on the marble countertop near the sink where he had been washing vegetables for the salad to go with dinner.

"You cooked?"

"Don't look so surprised. I eat a lot so of course I cook. Tonight is steak from my brother's ranch and twice baked potatoes."

A tiny furrow formed between Alex' eyes but it was gone as quickly as it appeared. "I wish I'd known you were cooking. I've already eaten."

Cane gave her a hard look. She was lying. She knew she was coming for dinner but he didn't want to fight about it. He hadn't seen her all week so he would leave that discussion for later. "More for me I guess."

Alex smiled as she slid off the counter. "So, no tour?"

Cane looked over at her. He had almost forgotten she had never been there before. She fit here, in his kitchen, in his house, in his life. "Sorry. Yeah, this is my kitchen." He gestured to the large open plan room.

Alex nodded as she looked around. "It's nice."

"Here, let me show you around. You have seen the kitchen and the entry hall."

"My apartment could fit in your entryway. Very understated, just like I would expect from you." Alex smiled.

"That's why we need to spend more time here. I barely fit in your apartment. How long is your lease?"

"Long enough," she responded as if she knew where this conversation was headed. Moving in together was the logical step. That is the direction they were going. That way they would at least see each other most days, even if in passing. Alex followed him from room to room.

"No football propaganda," Alex said as she sized up the walls.

"Nope. I get enough football at work."

146

Alex scrunched her nose again. "I wish my dad had the same philosophy. Everything in his house is OU football. Even the salt shakers. The house is a sea of maroon. Don't get me wrong, I love football, obviously, but I would like to have some shirts growing up that didn't have the OU logo on it."

"Is that why you picked UT, because they are OU's rival?"

"I already told you they have a better journalism school."

"There are lots of good journalism schools that aren't OU's rivals."

She thought for a second. "Maybe I needed a break from it, but mostly it was so I could stand on my own two feet. My dad is like royalty there. I have no doubt they will be building him a statue when he retires or name a building after him. He is great but I wanted to be Alex not coach Ambrose's daughter. At UT my dad's name didn't open any doors for me."

That was an understatement. No doubt, Alex had to work harder at UT because of her dad's reputation. They were getting dangerously close to feelings territory, where Alex usually shut him down, but Cane pushed further. "Is that why you don't want people to know about us? Because you don't want to just be Cane Clayburn's girlfriend."

"I don't want to be known as anyone's girlfriend."

"And yet, here we are. Someday you will be somebody's wife, not just a girlfriend." He was careful to say somebody, nothing specific, no pressure. It was fine to joke about marriage and kids but this was a serious conversation; one of their few.

"Someday I will probably need a root canal, too. I'm not going to dwell on that, either. Now come on, the Salvatore brothers wait for no man."

They went back to the kitchen. Cane dished himself a plate. "Want some salad at least?"

Alex glanced up from her phone. "No thanks, Corn Fed."

Cane frowned. He didn't want to eat in front of her if she wasn't going to join him but he would starve if he adopted an eat-only-when-Alex-eats policy. In the last month, they had not shared a single meal together. She was always "not hungry" or had "just eaten". It was bullshit. She was starving herself to look thinner on camera. He promised himself not to fight with her about it tonight but it was getting ridiculous. He was going to have to bring it up at some point. He had promised to be supportive but he could not support this. It wasn't healthy.

He cut into his steak to distract himself. "How was Connecticut?" he asked.

Alex nodded. "Connecticut is cold. And there aren't gun racks on the back of everyone's truck. It's weird, it's like nobody expects to go hunting on their way to the supermarket. Oh, and get this, not a single 'get ur dun' bumper sticker in the whole state. Oh…oh…oh and nobody says y'all."

"Sounds barbaric. I couldn't do it." Cane smiled but he realized Alex hadn't really answered the question. She never wanted to talk about what was happening at ESPN. At some point, she was going to be offered a job at their headquarters. They were trialing her. She never used those words but it was clear. The interview with Max Argyle had gotten their attention. If she wasn't offered an anchor job by the end of the season, he would be surprised. Cane tried to be happy for her, but he missed her as it was but at least now she was based in the same city. They were going to have that talk soon. He looked forward to that one about as much as he looked forward to talking to her about her new diet. He didn't want to fight. They got so little time together as it was. Cane finished his meal in silence.

"I also have the box set of *The Wire* if you would prefer to watch that," Cane said as he sat down on the couch.

Alex shook her head. "No way. We're doing this, Corn Fed." Alex sat down in the chair diagonal to the television. Cane shook his head and pointed to the couch.

"No, if we're watching, we're cuddling."

Alex made an exasperated noise but moved to sit beside him. He wrapped his arm around her and pulled her close. God, she felt good. Alex was at his house. He never thought he would enjoy something so simple as watching stupid shows. Before he met Alex, this would be on the top of his list of worst ways to spend a Friday night. He had always been a hit-it-then-quit-it type. Relationships were out of the question. God, he had been stupid. What an ass he was. A bizarre idea came to mind. What if he would have met Alex at UT? Hooked up with her then? He would have spared himself a lot of questionable decisions, and he would have had more time with her. He wished he could go back and speak to his college self, tell him to look out for the hot journalism major. He smiled at the thought.

"You're not even watching. You're staring at me." Alex's eyes darted at him.

"Cause you're beautiful." Cane pressed a kiss against her temple.

"So are the Salvatores. Now watch."

Cane glanced back at the TV. She was right, he had no idea what was going on and he didn't care, he was happy to just sit and hold her.

As if she was reading his mind, Alex tapped his chest. "You better start paying attention. There will be a test at the end."

Cane groaned. "Okay, catch me up. So, we have these two gay guys—"

Alex snapped her head around. "What gay guys? There are no gay guys."

Cane's eyes narrowed. Was she being serious? He paused the show. "Those two." He pointed at the screen. "Totally gay."

"They are brothers!"

He glanced at the screen. "And they're a couple? Well, that is just gross. What kind of shit do you watch, Alex? Next time, I'm picking."

"Arg, Corn Fed. You are managing to ruin *The Vampire Diaries* for me. Not cool." Alex stood up. "Let's have sex. That's one thing you can't ruin." She smiled as she offered him a hand to help him off the couch. Cane glanced at her jeans, they hung low on her hips, not because of the style but because they were too big. He pulled back the waist and read the tag. Before he could stop himself, he shook his head. He ran his hand over her ass. The curve was gone. Her butt wasn't just smaller, it had disappeared. The conversation couldn't wait.

"What happened to my friend?" Cane asked, patting her bottom. Alex grabbed his hand and tried to pull him up from the couch but he didn't budge. "How much do you weigh now?"

Alex dropped his hand. "Never ask a woman how much she weighs. That is boyfriend 101."

"You have gone down a size already. You were a six when we got together and now, you're in a four and they're too big."

Alex held up her hands. "The camera adds ten pounds."

He ignored her argument. He had heard it from her before. "Please tell me you have reached your target and you're not trying to lose any more."

Alex ignored him. "Take me to bed, Corn Fed." She smiled. She was trying to distract him with sex. And damn if it wasn't a solid strategy. The blood began diverting away from his head the moment he knew sex was on the table. Nope. Cane stood up. This needed to be addressed. His cock would hate him for this but it needed done.

"I have a surprise." He nodded with pride.

"Ooh, I like surprises. Am I going to need a safe word for this or anything? Should I start limbering up?"

Cane forced himself to look past her. Not going to be distracted. But God she was sexy. They could have this conversation after sex, or even during sex, he just needed to be inside her. He gave his head a hard shake to dislodge the thought. *Focus.*

"Remember our first date?"

"You mean my desk. I remember it well. I can't look at a stopwatch without getting wet. So, thanks for that, Corn Fed."

Cane smiled. Immediately the image of her on her desk, her legs spread so he could admire her pussy as he stroked her. He was a goner as soon as he touched her. Instantly he was hard. He was fighting a losing battle. Alex would be straddling him within a minute.

But that is what she wanted, to distract him. Cane took a step back. He couldn't be close to her right now, not without burying his cock deep in her.

"Perry's." His voice was strained. "Our first date was at Perry's."

"Yes. I remember watching you in the mirror when we had sex in the bathroom. Good times. I counted ten bathrooms when you gave me the tour. How long do you think it would take to christen every one?"

Cane took in a sharp breath. He had had the same thought after that night. Actually, he thought about how long it would take them to have sex in every room in his house. Yep, they would be doing that soon…but not until he finished the conversation.

"That night you ordered peanut butter cheesecake and when you were eating it you made the same sound you do when we have sex. So, I went in to Perry's today and bought you a cheesecake. Let's have dessert. And then we can burn off the calories." It was a challenge. He hoped she would accept it. She needed to start eating normally again.

Alex moved toward him. Her hands went to his zipper. "Or you can eat it off me. We can skip the bathroom sex and start with kitchen counter sex."

His cock sprung out when she unzipped his pants. Alex worked over his hard length. He would stop her in a minute. But God it felt good. It had been too long. Every day he stroked himself and pretended it was her, but it was nowhere near as good. Just a few more seconds. Alex lowered her head. Her tongue licked around the crown, pulling him into her mouth. Oh fuck, that was good. She knew exactly how he liked it. Her hands cupped his balls as she sucked. He laced his fingers through her dark hair. He would come like this. A few more minutes and he would be coming down her throat.

Somewhere in the back of his mind, a voice told him she was doing this just to distract him. He didn't care. It felt too good to stop. But the voice got louder. He needed to speak to her. This is one of the times where Alex needed a push. With a pained groan, Cane pulled away.

Alex's head snapped up; her eyes wide with surprise. "What's wrong? Did I hurt you?"

"God no. The opposite of that." He didn't want to stop the physical intensity of his enjoyment with Alex, but he had to stop and address the physical demise of her body.

"What did you eat today?"

Alex blinked a few times. "What?"

"What have you had to eat? What did you have for dinner?"

"I have eaten."

"What, tell me what you have eaten."

Alex's eyes flashed with defiance. "No. It doesn't matter."

For a long moment silence reigned, neither of them willing to relinquish any ground. "Fine," Cane said eventually. "Let's go to bed."

Alex visibly relaxed. She thought he was dropping it. Best she learned now that he was just as stubborn as her. You don't make it to his level in sports by having a weak will.

Cane stripped down to his boxers. Usually, he slept naked but he was going to need all the help he could get. He forced himself to look away when Alex got undressed. Strong. Iron will. Then he made the mistake of looking up just as she slipped his jersey on. Fuck. She knew what that did to him. Nope. Not tonight. He let out a stream of air.

Cane waited for Alex to climb into bed before he turned off the lights.

"Good night, Alex. See you in the morning."

Alex reached out and stroked his chest. "Forget the morning."

Cane turned Alex over until she was facing away from him and then pulled her against his chest, pinning her arms in place so she could not touch him. He had an iron will but he was also a man with a beautiful willing woman in his bed.

"Good night, Alex," he said again through clenched teeth. "We're not having sex again until you start eating."

"What?" Alex tried to squirm out of his embrace but he held her firmly against him.

"Good night, Alex." It was his turn to not want to talk. She needed to go to sleep or eat something and then climb on top of him; those were the two choices. He didn't have time for anything else.

"Why am I here if we're not going to have sex?" She sounded clearly surprised.

Not nearly as surprised as him. He was forgoing sex with the woman he loved because it was the best thing for her. How fucking ridiculous was that? His temples pounded. Great, now he had a headache and a massive erection, two of the things least conducive to sleep. "Because I want a healthy girlfriend more than I want sex."

"Your penis is poking me in the back."

"I know. And if you keep moving, I will come on your back." He didn't mean to sound pissed, but he *was* pissed. This is not how he expected his weekend to go. He had not seen Alex for a week and all he wanted to do was be deep inside of her. Not be hard on the outside.

"Do you want me to go home?"

"No. I want you to eat a slice of cheesecake and then ride me."

Alex laughed. "You are ridiculous. Have I ever told you that?"

"Once a day since we met."

"I'm not going to eat cheesecake this weekend. Just so we're clear. I don't want you holding out hope for that. This is my chance, Cane. I have one shot. I need to grab it with both hands."

"Alex you're so smart and so fucking sexy. Of course, they will want you. But why do you want to work somewhere you have to starve yourself to fit in? I'm not okay with that. We're together now and my job is to look after you even if it pisses you off."

Alex was quiet for a long time. He thought she might have fallen asleep but eventually she said,

"You're a good man, Corn Fed." She pressed a kiss to his knuckles.

Cane smiled. She didn't give in but she didn't fight him; that was progress. He would claim that one as a victory. Should he press his luck? Probably not but he would.

"Come home with me for Thanksgiving. My family wants to meet you."

Alex stiffened. "I can't. I always go to the OU game so I can be with my dad. Ever since I was a kid, I have sat on the bench with him. I love it. Thanksgiving has always meant hot dogs and nachos and hanging out with my dad."

"You've never had turkey, and pumpkin pie on Thanksgiving? That is just sad."

"No, it's not. We just have a different tradition than you." Her body moved back.

Cane pulled her in closer. "Traditions change. You're coming home with me. Next year we'll go to the OU game. Those are words I never thought I would ever utter. Look at us. We are nailing this couple thing."

"Well, we're certainly not nailing each other." She let her head nestle in his arms.

"Eat the cheesecake and we will be, sweetheart."

Alex rubbed her ass along the length of his cock. "Good night, Corn Fed."

Fuck! It was going to be a long night.

CHAPTER SEVENTEEN

It was too late to call on a non-game night. She knew his phone would already be put away. She rarely sent a text but she needed to begin the conversation. Thanksgiving was only a week away. Never in a million years had she thought this type of conversation would happen. She was torn. Alex took in a deep breath and began to type.

"So, for Thanksgiving, Cane asked if I would spend it with his family." Her left pinky tapped the send button too soon. Arg. Alex contemplated what next to type. She glanced back on the field. The Texans were up by ten points and with only forty-five seconds left in the game. Cane was at the line. His whole body was intense and focused. He signaled a play and the center snapped the ball.

The world was in slow motion. Chavaz came up from the right but that damn slacky Austin was nowhere. Why was he even on the field? She could have done a better job. It made no sense. Chavez charged hard. Cane passed the ball down the field to Calandrino who caught it at the twenty-yard line as another player from the defense pulled him down. He held tight to the ball. It was complete. Alex cut her eyes to Cane as Chavez hit him hard from his blindside. Cane went down with a thud that rattled in Alex's brain. It was a precise hit to his left shoulder. The shoulder that had been injured. The part of his body that required extensive surgery and recovery. *No. No. Not his shoulder.* Alex gasped and raised her hand to her mouth. She stepped forward and Alistair grabbed her arm.

"You can't," he warned.

"He's hurt."

"Don't go out there. You aren't allowed on the field yet." He cocked his head and stared down at her. "You know this." The look in his eyes commanded her not to take another step. Alex didn't want to take a step. She wanted to run. She needed to hear Cane's voice. If she heard his voice, she knew she would be able to tell how badly he was hurt. But from the sidelines she was like everyone else... a spectator to this game and him.

Alex bit her lip and stood in place. Desperation pushed down on the pedal of adrenaline in her mind. It had amplified through her veins as she waited on the sidelines with everyone else. The pound of blood that throbbed inside of her roared over the crowd. Even if she had forgone all sense of reality and rules of life and rushed onto the field it wouldn't have been possible. Any attempt to cross the green and she would have been stopped by a ref. Air evacuated from her lungs and pain pulsated through her chest. *Breathe. Breathe.* She forced herself to exhale. It stung. Dammit. Of course, it was his blindside. Why was she the only one that called this? Well other sports commentators had as well, but why hadn't his coach done something about it? Why hadn't Cane made him do it? Now he was lying on the field. In pain. Cane was hurt. Pain ran through her own veins. It wasn't physical it was emotional. The idea of the man she cared so much for was in pain. *Cared.* No. It was more than that. God, it was so much more than that. She hadn't said it but he knew. He let her dance around the edges of the word. Allowing her to come close but not commit to the four letters. Just stick her toe in and test the idea of it. He protected her heart for her, now. He hadn't before. But he did now. She swallowed hard. Cane's massive muscular body had been flat on his back too long.

The stretcher came out onto the field. Cane waved them off and struggled to get to his feet. He motioned to everyone and the team to set up again. *Are you crazy?* What was he doing? He was injured. Cane needed to be off the field and under the care of a physician, not with his team on the field ready for the next play. Alex scanned the time clock. There were twenty seconds left and zero timeouts. The Texans had technically already won the game. There was no need to continue. "Please take a knee," she whispered. "Do not run the play." From the distance, Alex could only view Cane's face from the big screen. His eyes were like icicles. Almost clear. Like ice from the first freeze of winter. Why was he doing this? It was obvious he had channeled all of his physical strength just to stand up and finish the play. Alex swallowed.

Her phone buzzed. It was her dad. He was up? *"Sounds good, have fun. Tell Cane they need to fire Austin. He is the worst left tackle in the league."* Alex jerked her head back. The game. He saw it. She bit her lip.

"I can't believe he is back up." She shook her head. Alex wished she could shake some sense into him. He did not belong on the field right now.

As she placed her phone back in her pocket it vibrated. *"He's a good quarterback. One of the best in the nation. But he is going to be out for the next game. He was down too long. He's in pain."*

Shit. He was right. This was so bad. Cane threw the ball down the field and Calandrino made it to the end zone. They scored. Game. Good. Cane made his way to the sideline.

Now she was supposed to interview him and not show her emotions. *Okay. Do it. Be a professional. Call it like it is.*

The crowd was on their feet and players were rushing the field but Alex could only see Cane. Damn it. He was hurt. A lump formed in her throat but she swallowed it.

"Alex Martin reporting on the sideline with Cane Clayburn. Cane, great game. The last touchdown wasn't necessary and a bit of a risk. Why didn't you take a knee?"

Cane's eyes were so clear. Good grief he was in pain. His face was free from any lines. Smooth and without expression. He was obviously focused on doing the interview. He forced a laugh. "There is only one time in my life where I will take a knee."

Whether or not this was true, Cane had lived up to this stat to date, he always played out the game. Always. It was a message for her. Alex was sure of it. It didn't matter. This was not anything she was concerned with in this moment. Anger filled her mind. She couldn't get past his shoulder and his damn blindside not being covered. Alex bit her lip. *Don't say it. Don't cross the line.*

"Is Coach Grisham intentionally trying to have you injured by keeping Austin on the field when everyone with an IQ over eighty can see that he does not have your blindside covered?"

Cane blinked and shook his head. Yes, she stepped over the boundaries of comfortable questions but it needed to be asked and someone needed to answer. No more soft balls. This was real. Cane had been seriously injured and probably still was, but was not going to show it. At least not on the field.

"So, is that a, yes?" She pushed the mic toward his mouth. The lips that had been all over her body and then some. Alex loved being on the sidelines with a camera behind her but in this instance, it would be so much better if they were in bed. It had been a week since they had been together. After his cheesecake sex refusal, Alex was so sexually frustrated she couldn't even bring *herself* to orgasm completely. The surge would trickle down her legs like a faucet that needed to be fixed and then nothing. It was awful. This never happened to her. She was a woman that got it done. Every time.

"Come on Alex, are you seriously throwing me that low

ball question? You're better than that." His brows furrowed.

Alex took in a deep breath. "It's not low ball. I'd say it was the perfect pass and if you were the running back, I think the refs would say it was an incomplete."

Cane laughed. "I always finish. You know that."

Her eyes bulged. Alex swallowed. She couldn't believe he had outed them. And on live TV. Alex tossed her hair over her shoulders as if she could flip off the switch of her emotions for Cane.

She smiled. Time to up the ante. Two could play at this game. This wasn't football with twenty-two players on the field. It was Cane and Alex and a million television viewers.

"Do I?" *There, I answered the question. Let's see how you respond. How does it feel to be called out live?*

Cane nodded. "Yes, sweetheart, you do. Thanks for the chat." He pushed past her.

Alex's cheeks were on fire. She cut her eyes to Alistair. He nodded at her to answer the question. Yes, it was live. Yes, it had been recorded. Yes, everyone that had their television on would have seen it. And if they hadn't it would be reshared over and over. There was no need to check the Socials there was no doubt they would be on the only hashtags. Alex swallowed and followed through with the last of her sideline interviews and exited the stadium.

***

They hadn't made plans. It was more of an assumption they would get together after the game. But Alex was not in the mood to have a visit from Cane. She turned her phone off. Took a shower and jumped in bed. He could enjoy the sound of her voicemail. There would be no return calls tonight. No texts. No sex. Nothing. Alex was mortified. Humiliated. This was so not cool. Her career was important to her and he had jeopardized it. She was not going to be a sideline joke. Alex wanted to be an anchor. It was in sight and the interview with Cane would be a setback not a step forward. So many yards had been gained and his comment would no doubt be at least a five-yard penalty. Her head hit the pillow with a thud and her mind went to Cane and his shoulder. *Drop it.* They could tackle that issue in the morning. Not tonight. Tonight, she would sleep and shut out everything and everyone.

***

At six a.m. Alex turned her phone back on and it vibrated for a good twenty minutes. Between being tagged on all the socials and the texts from Vanessa, Kasia, Hailee, Mason, the list was too long. And yet not long enough. There was one name that was not in her messages. One name that had not called. *Seriously? He didn't call? Really?* No, he was not ghosting her. Absolutely not. She was being the ghoster. She had intentionally ghosted him. All of her pride and satisfaction twisted into a tight ball and secured itself in the back of her throat. Why hadn't he reached out? He was the one that had messed up not her. He outed them. On television. While she was at work. That wasn't okay, at all. But seriously nothing? She had imagined him at her door with flowers and chocolate. Or eighty thousand texts and missed calls.

And yet there was zero. Nothing. Not even a "GM". Fear began to run through her mind.

Why? Why hadn't he tried? The lump in the back of her throat dropped like a rollercoaster that had inched its way to the top of the mountain and slammed down with gravity and sheer force of being pushed to a place no one wanted to go. The place that wreaks of pain and despair, of missed hopes and possibilities. It was worse given that she had been shown such a shiny gorgeous location. Alex had been turnkey about Cane from the get go but now, after everything, she was ready to sit down and discuss the contract. And as if pure poetry she let go of everything in the past and was ready to sit at the table with her heart, and now there was nothing to discuss. He had ghosted her.

No, technically he hadn't ghosted her. Neither of them had reached out. Neither had avoided a call but neither of them had made one either. Alex took in a deep breath and her stomach sunk further. He had been so concerned about her weight. It was sweet. It didn't matter she would continue to lose weight but his words had played against her heart, regardless. Alex pulled up her text message.

"I should bench you." She hit send without a consideration as to whether or not it was a worthy enough text and self-worth was not exactly a focus in her brain at the moment. Alex missed Cane. Even though she wanted to be the one that was mad and have him grovel back to her good graces. The fact that he hadn't reached out caved in the walls of emotions deep inside of her. It was like freshman college year all over again. She had been filled with self-doubt and for one tiny moment he had made her think and believe in a fantasy that did not exist. And here she was again the one on the chase.

She glanced at her phone. Nothing. She wasn't going to let this go. Not yet. She texted him again.

"The fine increases with each minute that you don't respond."

Time to shower off some of this distraction. The water was hot and it almost seemed as if she could wash off the doubt and disbelief from her skin. Except this relationship had passed the first level. Alex had fought it at every step but they were in a relationship and she didn't want it to end. Even if it were for naught, she would throw a Hail Mary into the end zone for Cane. She wanted to.

It was Columbus Day. Time to carpe diem and drop the anchor. She was ready to do it. They both had the day off. Cane would be at home. Alex was sure of it. He was injured. This might even be the reason he hadn't responded. His phone might be dead and he could be in pain. Several months ago, she had joked to Vanessa and Kasia about costumes for Vanessa's annual Halloween party. One night after several bottles of wine, Alex had ordered a sexy doctor outfit. It was a bit of a buzzed decision. But it would be perfect for today. She sorted through her clothes and found the package. It was a light blue dress that zipped up the front and red lace over the top of her breasts. Even if Cane had decided against them, he wouldn't be able to resist her in this outfit…at least they would have one final moment of pleasure. Her heart sank. Alex didn't want a final moment of pleasure. She could do this. *Yes.* The dress slid over her body. Yeah. No way was she going to leave her apartment like this. She threw on his jersey over the top of the costume. It didn't matter who saw at this point. He had already claimed her on the field when he tackled Marquez and then pointed out that he always finished in last night's interview. If anything, and given her texts from the studio, they loved the interview. This would be more fodder for them. So be it. She didn't care. All Alex cared about was Cane and his arms. His shoulder. She needed to make sure he was okay. She doubted that he was. Alex swallowed. Fear brewed along her skin with the notion of his silence being more about him than her or them combined. It rose to the very core of how much he could be in pain. The risk of his career being over. Physically, emotionally, Cane had to be in a bad place and Alex was going to go to him and make it better. This is what people in relationships do. She knew this. He had always mentioned what he had read about how things work as a couple, but Alex didn't need a guideline for Cane. She just needed him.

With a deep breath she pushed the button down on her window. This moment was one she had never foreseen for herself. But this was his comfort food. Obviously. It's what Cane ate when he needed to retreat in the pleasures of the mouth. Not the sexual part, the food part. Alex did, too. Or at least, she had prior to the on-air position. But now, she would take out her frustration and seek out all her pleasures from him.

"Hi, can I get a bucket of chicken, the mashed potatoes and biscuits, please?"

"Sure thing, pull up to the window."

Thank everything and anyone it was a window and she didn't have to get out of her car to face the staff and or anyone else as she bought the breaded and fried, calorie laden, cholesterol heart attack feast. She blinked her eyes and blew out a deep breath. Still no texts. What was that about? Maybe this was a game or one of his relationship shoves. He continued to hike them down the line. Make her take another step. Maybe that was the radio silence.

Alex parked in the extended driveway of Cane's house. With the food in one hand and his jersey as a camouflage for her sexy doctor costume she made her way to the door. Her knuckles paused for a second. Should she even be here?

Yes.

Her hand made a solid touchdown against the steel. Nothing. How long had she been here? Zero response? What the hell? Alex stamped her foot. This was not real. No way. She rummaged through her purse and found her phone. The dial tone rang for three seconds.

"Corn Fed, are you wanting to be benched?" She blew off the hair that had settled on her brow.

"I can't talk right now."

Alex blinked her eyes. "What? I'm outside your door. Let me in."

"It's not a good time."

"Corn Fed, you better open this door or we will not be having words. There will be zero words. Like ever. Didn't your mama raise you better? You do not ignore a woman on your doorstep with food."

Eventually the door opened. Cane's face appeared slightly deflated. He had an ice pack attached to his shoulder with gauze. Shit. He was in pain. Alex winced.

"I'm sorry, I shouldn't have said anything about your mama. That was not nice." Alex stepped into his entryway.

"Yea, wait till she hears about it. She's not exactly your biggest fan as it is."

Alex's heart sank. "Why not? I'm not barefoot pregnant

material?"

A smile crossed Cane's face. It was slight, barely enough to pull the sides of his mouth up. God, he was really in pain. That's why he hadn't responded. He didn't want her to know. Alex was sure of it.

"You're definitely barefoot pregnant material but my mama is not keen…it doesn't matter. I'm not going to be much fun today. I have to run through some videos. How about we reschedule?"

Alex's chest tightened. *Breathe.* No way. Not happening. "Did you forget who I was? I like videos. I watch videos on the daily. Hello?"

Cane pressed his lips together and shook his head. "My method is really boring. I won't be good company today, okay?" He kissed her head as if he could send her off and she would go. No. She wasn't some fangirl. He was the one that wanted this relationship. He pushed for it. He made her break her only rule about him and now he wanted to shut it down? No. This was not how this was going to go. No. It couldn't.

"Cane, I'm in your jersey. I've brought over a bucket of chicken and other heart attack inducing food and you are showing me the door? Sorry, but not sorry. I'm not leaving. I'm staying. Consider yourself pushed into the end zone. I'm not going to fumble on this play in our relationship." She swallowed. "You're hurt and you want to be alone. I get it. But I'm not going to do that. I'm going to imprint myself against your skin and you will like it. No. You will enjoy it. Even better, this day will be one you look back on when you are on an away game and I'm not reporting from the sidelines because you will be alone in your hotel and you will be wanting me." She tapped his chest with her pointer finger.

"You can stay. You are welcome in my house always. But I'm not talking." He made his way to the couch and sat down in front of the wide screen television. It was paused on the sack that had injured him.

Alex pulled the jersey off over her head. "That's fine. This doctor is happier with the silent patient that doesn't add in their own research input. I know what I'm doing. So, sit back and enjoy my expertise."

"Doctor? That looks like a naughty nurse." He let out a sharp breath. "To me."

"Of course, that's what it looks like to you. Because you are a sexist macho man. But if you notice this outfit is green. I'm not a nurse. I'm a doctor. Please study up on cos-play outfits, this won't be your last rodeo."

Cane shook his head. "Never mention rodeo again pre-sex."

"What? Why?"

"Again, sweetheart do your research. Cord, my youngest brother is a rodeo cowboy. So, no rodeo references pre or during sex." He slapped her behind.

She jumped. "Oh, but you like to smack it. That works for me. Oh, no. I dropped the needle." Alex bent over in front of Cane and pretended to search for the imaginary object. His hands ran over her ass like he was a health inspector at a grocery store and needed to decide which produce was safe. Alex was more than safe and ready.

His hands cupped her ass. "Alex, stop losing weight. I miss your ass. This is a smaller representation of what we had. The big and beautiful."

"You sound like a soap opera."

"I wish I was and I would kill your evil twin that is making you do things to your body that shouldn't be happening." He massaged her behind and kissed her cheeks.

Alex turned around. "I brought you some chicken in a bucket."

"Good, because this isn't happening unless you eat some with me." He swatted her behind.

"I already ate."

"Right." He laced his fingers together and pressed his lips together.

"Again? Seriously?" She let out a deep sigh.

"Fine." Alex made her way to the kitchen and popped the lid off the chicken. Fried and greasy. This was going to take serious mind over matter. Even if she hadn't been on a strict celery diet this would never be something she would eat. Fried chicken from a bucket? Gross. It was the epitome of trashy food. Like why have a guy with black specs as the logo instead of a racoon, that would make more sense?

Arg. Alex picked up the smallest drumstick and took a bite.

"Happy?" Alex waved the bone in front of Cane's face. He leaned down and took a bite from the piece of chicken she held.

"Very. There is nothing sexier than you in that nurse's costume eating KFC." He took another bite.

"Doctor."

"Yes, Nurse Alex?"

She rolled her eyes and gave him a shove. He captured her fingers. "I've missed you."

Alex's lungs squeezed tight. She had missed him, too. More than she had ever missed anyone. She was all in. It was official. No other definition would work. Those four letters that spelled the one emotion Alex didn't want to have with Cane. Not him. Not again. She couldn't do it. But yet, she was. She was there in that place. The destination everyone wants to achieve. The special spot which encompasses everything that makes sense. Everything that makes a bad day turn from blue to green. There was no way to turn back. The dam had been broken and she was not able to hold back anymore. Even if it meant the four letters would not follow the three-letter acronym Alex really wanted. She hoped. God, she hoped it was possible. But there was doubt. How could there not be? Alex sucked in air like she was able to take in more than her fair share of oxygen and overcompensate for the emotions that zinged all over her body. Her love. Yes, love. It radiated for him.

"Well, nothing says true love like going against your personal standards and being seen buying chicken in a bucket." Thank goodness no one had seen her or at least she wasn't hashtagged on the socials, yet.

"Is that your way of saying it?" Cane tipped up her chin so Alex had to face him and his question.

She bit her lip. A final pause before she let her guard down. "Saying what?"

"Saying you love me. Alex, you don't have to be afraid. It's three one syllable words. No need to consult the thesaurus I gave you." He pulled her in close and his lips grazed against her ear. "I love you, Alex."

A waterfall of icicles spread over the back of her neck and down through her body. He said it. First. How long had she waited and anticipated or dreamed about this moment? Too many to count. It was ridiculous. And here it was vivid and true. He did love her. It was so real it crashed from his mouth onto her skin and deeper as it reached the shores of self-doubt and self-worth and cascaded into this beautiful enclosure where only two people can meet together. It's a special effect on the soul no one can capture on film the way it rings with authenticity in your heart. It is so much more than a visualization. It is an experience that can't be bought or faked. Only when both people are all in and forego their guards do the colors of this emotion shine through. And what a fucking glorious sight. It's filled with every single color of the rainbow and it hurts. It's so good it hurts. Like doing squats or after a finished marathon. Your body is sore and has to side step down the stairs but being in that place is so much more than the pain. It is bigger than everything. And once you have visited this destination, you don't ever want to leave.

Alex raised her eyes to meet Cane's. "I do love you Cane, which is why I bought you chicken in a bucket. Now, no more telling and more showing. I ate the chicken. Give me my reward."

A smile crossed Cane's face. "You what now?"

"Yes, I love you. Even if your career was over, I would love you. There is so much more to you than football." She poked his chest.

His eyes dropped. Shit. She shouldn't have said that. He was too hurt to deal with the idea of no football. Even though that day would arrive with or without injury. At some point he would retire.

"Corn Fed, don't go soft on me now. I've given more than ever. Reward me."

Cane shook his head. "Nurse Alex, we've had some complaints about you lately."

"From who?"

"A patient. He doesn't like the lack of extra care he used to get." He pulled on the zipper of her dress. Alex inhaled as he tugged it all the way down. The sleeves of the costume slipped over her shoulder. She had gone without any type of undergarment. Cane raised an eyebrow and flexed a vein in his throat as he gazed at her bare breasts.

"Maybe it's a point of view difference and the patient was the one not willing to go with the prescribed treatment." Her dress and knees dropped to the ground simultaneously. She grasped his cock and stroked it with a downward and twist repetition. Down and twist. Down and twist.

Alex's mouth lowered to his erection as she took him in past her lips and further down her throat. Deeper. It didn't matter how deep he went. Alex would take all of him. He could reach the depths of her body. Go for it. She was ready. Go deep. Deep throat her to the point of no return. All barricades had been dropped and the only thing Alex was concerned with was mutual pleasure. Down and twist with her mouth. Down and twist. Alex's fingers grasped Cane's balls and rubbed them nice and slow applying pressure. Each round. Each circle. Each stroke. Faster. Harder. Deeper. All of him. Alex deep throated Cane until a creamy, salty taste drizzled down her throat. Satisfaction flowed over her body. There. She gave it to him. God, she wanted to give it to him every single day. He encompassed everything that Alex wanted and needed. She was in deep…Love.

CHAPTER EIGHTEEN

"Did you know they make vegan butter?" Alex scrunched her nose as she examined the pie she had just pulled out of the oven. 'They do," she answered her own question, "and it's not the same as margarine. That shiz does not bake well, apparently. Can you tell those are supposed to be leaves? I should have gone with the classic pinch crust. There is a reason it has classic in the title. Arg. Do I have time to start again?" Alex eyed the clock above the oven.

She brushed her hands against the sides of her legs. It was time to leave for Cut and Shoot but Alex had still not had a shower or packed her bag. She had insisted on sleeping at her own apartment last night so she could practice making pies. In the entire time he had known Alex, she had not made a single meal or expressed any sort of desire to bake but she was determined to make the *perfect pecan pie* for Thanksgiving. Cane put his bag on the floor. They would not be leaving anytime in the near future. He knew that look, Alex's getting-shit-done look. There would be no stopping her until she was done.

"They all look great. And no, you don't have time to bake another pie. We need to leave."

Alex stood on her tiptoes and pressed a chaste kiss to his

lips. "I missed you, Corn Fed. You should have stayed here last night. I needed a taste tester."

"Which body part? They all taste great. Want me to show you?"

Alex flicked him with a rolled-up dish towel. "Save your sexual harassment for later, I have a serious pie situation here."

Cane tried not to smile but failed. She was taking meeting his family very seriously. Like everything else in her life, Alex was determined to do this well. He didn't have the heart to tell her that the Clayburns were pumpkin pie people.

Alex pointed to the pie furthest from him. "I need you to taste this. I really wish you were here last night to taste it because now it is too late." Alex didn't wait. She took a spoon and dug into the center of the pie. "Here taste this." She pushed the spoon to his lips. "What do you think?"

"Mmm," Cane said after he swallowed. "It's great. Now go take a shower and get dressed."

Alex's eyes narrowed. "Are you just saying it is good or is it goood? You won't hurt my feelings. It's not a family recipe or anything. I got it from a romance novel of all places. Great book by the way. Gave it three stars. I loved it." She batted her eyelashes at him.

Cane shook his head. "The pie is great. Giving a book you like three stars is weird, but the pie is fine. Now let's go."

"I hardly ever give above three stars. Three is I loved it. Four is I want to take the book home to meet my friends and family and five means it's my one and only and I will never love a book as much as that book." She took in a deep breath. "What do you mean, fine?"

"It's good. Now get in the shower."

"Good, great and fine. You have used three different adjectives. Which is it?" Alex put her hands on her hips and gave him a hard stare.

Cane chose his words wisely. "I give it a ...three." That

was Alex's idea of good, right?

Alex nodded. "A three." She bit her lip. "I need at least a four here." With another fork she dug into a second piece. "Try again and really try and experience it like you weren't worried about me jumping in the shower." She stuffed the pie in his mouth.

"Yes, definitely a four." Cane nodded.

Alex's shoulders dropped. "Okay, that's good. We can work with that. What do I need to do to push it up to a five? Would you go with the rope, pinch, or leaf crust?" Alex gestured to the table. She had made five pies plus the one he had just sampled.

"Alex my mama said not to bring anything. We're good. Any pie you bring is extra. Between her and Cheyenne, there will be enough food to last until the second coming. Now let's go."

Alex kept nodding but she wasn't listening. "It needs ice cream. No. Cool Whip, it needs Cool Whip. Yes. That's what it needs."

"Okay, I'm sure my mama has Cool Whip."

Alex tapped her lips with her finger. "Nope, ice cream. It needs vanilla Bluebell."

"My mama has that, too," Cane lied. He had no idea what his mom had but he did know that if they were late, Alex would have absolutely no hope of winning his mom over.

The announcement that he was bringing Alex home was met with some opposition from his mom. A lot actually. The words "over my dead body" may have been uttered. Cane didn't bother fighting. He knew his mom. There was no coming back from the articles Alex had written. Katrina Clayburn forgot nothing. His mother would be civil. Manners were paramount for her, but she would make sure Alex knew exactly how she felt. Cane groaned inwardly. He briefly considered cancelling and going to Oklahoma with Alex. The very fact that he was willing to sit through an OU game told him everything he needed to know. He loved

Alex, really loved her and he needed her to be comfortable with his family. His family was everything to him. He wanted Alex to be part of that. He wanted her to see Cut and Shoot as her home, too.

"Alex we're going to be late." Cane rubbed his chin.

"What? The game doesn't start until four."

"Sweetheart, there is more to Thanksgiving than football. I told my mama we would be there by noon."

Alex's eyes widened. "You what now? You didn't tell me this. And I know there is more to Thanksgiving. Hello. Did you not see the pies?" Alex unbuttoned her shirt and took down her ponytail in preparation for her shower. "But we are watching football, right?"

The edge of panic in her voice made him smile. "You can watch football." He didn't tell her that the entire house would be rooting against OU no matter who they were playing. Forty minutes later they were ready to go. Alex wore a blue dress with a thin gold belt. "You look great," Cane said as he put her bag in the back of his silver Range Rover.

Alex smiled. "Thanks. It's been a while since I did a meet the family." She buckled her seatbelt before taking out a notepad. "Okay, Corn Fed, let's review. Oldest brother is Case. Went to Texas A&M. He is a vet." Alex looked over to him for confirmation.

"Yep, Case is the oldest and the smartest and probably the nicest." Cane put the car in to reverse.

"Arg, now you tell me. I got the wrong Clayburn." She scribbled on her notepad.

Cane had to laugh. "You're definitely not his type, sweetheart."

Alex's nose scrunched but she kept going. "Next is Colt. Rich cattle baron type. Owns the Night Latch. Married to Cheyenne Ford. One son named Garron."

Cane nodded. "Did I tell you Garron's name?"

"No. People magazine told me. I did research last night while the pies were baking."

"You could have just spent the night at my house and asked me."

"I'm not going to cheat on my research by asking you." She somehow managed to sound appalled at the suggestion.

"You know it's not really cheating since we are a couple. You can just ask me things now. One of the many perks of being my girlfriend."

"Many." Alex laughed. "Orgasms and always being able to spot you in a crowd are the only perks I know about. Are there more? Have you been holding out on me, Corn Fed?"

"That pretty much sums them up."

"Good thing those are two of my favorites. If I didn't already love you, I would have when we got separated at HEB. Everyone in Texas was shopping last night but I could always spot you. The tall blond guy, a head above everyone else, yep that one's mine. Now stop distracting me. The baby of the family is Cord, the rodeo cowboy. And of course, your mama, Katrina. Nurse and widow. Boom. I have learned them all. Anything else I should know?"

"That pretty much covers it." Cane smiled. Alex was all in. Like everything in her life, she committed fully. Whatever she did, she did well. And now she was committed to him, to being in a relationship. The turning point had been when he reinjured his shoulder. He shut down and pulled away but Alex pushed through. When he needed her, she came. He didn't even know he needed her, but he did. And she had not left him since. He hadn't played again since the injury but he would. He would be back to finish the season. But if he couldn't, he would still be okay because he had Alex. It would hurt.

He always knew his football career might have a short shelf life but now he could imagine a life after the NFL and it looked pretty good. It would be Alex travelling from city to city to report on games. That made him smile. Hotel sex was going to be part of their relationship for a long time to come. She should have spent the night with him. They needed to figure out a long-term situation. The back and forth was not something he intended to keep going.

Alex pulled out her phone. "I need to text my dad. This is our thing. We always text on game day. No calls. But usually, I am in the stands on Thanksgiving." The sides of her mouth pulled down but she quickly covered with a tight smile.

"Next year we will go to the OU game and eat hot dogs and nachos."

"Really?"

"Yes, really. Why are you surprised? Of course; that's what couples do; they take turns being tormented by the other person's traditions. So, this year, Thanksgiving with my people, Christmas with yours. Next year we will switch it up."

"Did you just invite yourself to Christmas at my dad's house?"

"He could always come to Houston and celebrate with us."

Alex's nose scrunched the way it did when he said something she disagreed with. "My apartment is too small."

They would be living together at his house by Christmas. Alex didn't know that yet, but they would be. Cane had his eye on the long game. He had started small by clearing out a drawer for her and buying her a toothbrush to keep at his house. Alex had yet to actually put anything in the drawer. She always brought an overnight bag. The toothbrush had also yet to be used because Alex had a supply of travel toothbrushes, she had stockpiled from every hotel stay. The toothbrush stash had replaced the condom stash in her top drawer. But eventually she would work her way through the supply and then she would have to use the one he had bought her, then bam, halfway to cohabitation.

"Ever notice Texas gets so much more picturesque when you leave Houston?" Alex looked out the window and sighed.

"Yeah, I've noticed. That's why I am building a house in Cut and Shoot."

Alex's head snapped around. "You are?"

"Yeah. I want to be closer to my family. It will be nice." Cane glanced over at her. He was going to say it would be nice when they had kids but instead, he said, "I want to raise my family there." Cane had stopped teasing her about marriage and children when their relationship got serious but they were going to have to have a proper discussion about it sometime.

"That's cool. It seemed nice. I mean, if you like tiny Texan towns."

"Doesn't everybody?" Alex was being too non-committal. She needed a push.

Alex shook her head. "No, Corn Fed. That is a niche market. So, I hope you really love this house you're building because resale would no doubt be a challenge."

Cane sighed. Either she didn't get what he was asking or she didn't want to respond. Either way he wasn't going to push the issue right before she met his mom.

Cane pulled onto the dirt road that led to his childhood home. Alex was staring out the window taking in the surroundings.

"Main street was cute. It looks like something out of a Western." Alex giggled.

"Cute. Exactly what the founders were going for. I'm pretty sure that is part of the motto."

"Is this your mom's house?" Alex beamed.

"This is it." Cane's hands were suddenly slick. Why was he nervous? He pulled at his collar. Thank God he was only going to have to do the meet the family thing once. "It's a nice place to live." He took out their bags.

Alex stopped at the front door. "Wow! I love her porch. How many girls did you kiss on this porch? No, don't tell me. There are some things a woman should never know. Let's pretend I never asked that."

Cane gathered Alex against his chest and lowered his mouth to hers. "You're the first." His lips brushed hers with every syllable. "And the last." He kissed her hard. Alex wrapped her arms around his neck and pulled him closer. Her mouth opened for him.

"Ahem."

Alex jumped out of his embrace. She pushed against him so hard she stumbled back. Cane righted her just before she fell.

"Hey mama." Cane smiled. "This is Alex. Alex this is my mom."

Alex's cheeks burned red. She smoothed out an imaginary wrinkle in her dress before she reached her hand out. "Nice to meet you, Mrs. Clayburn."

His mother hesitated for a moment before she took Alex's hand. There was a slight scowl on his mother's face, an expression Cane was not used to seeing. Katrina Clayburn had never met a stranger. She literally could not walk down the street without making a friend. She loved everyone, unless of course you hurt one of her own and then God help you. "Welcome to Cut and Shoot."

Cane put the bags down. "Which room are we staying in?"

"You're staying in your room. And Alex is staying in Colt's old room."

Cane nodded. Of course, his mama was putting them in separate rooms. She would put them in separate states if given the option.

Cane and Alex followed Katrina upstairs to put the bags down.

"You have a beautiful home." Alex gleamed at Katrina.

Katrina responded with a tight smile as she eyed Alex from head to toe, inspecting her. She was making absolutely no effort to make Alex feel comfortable. The atmosphere was palpable. Cane held in what would have been a long sigh. This was going to be a long weekend.

"Thank you for inviting me. I appreciate it." Alex began again. Bless her; she was trying. Alex had committed to making this work and she was doing her best. Sadly, his mother was a formidable opponent.

Katrina took a measured breath. "It's just a shame you aren't with your parents. I am sure they would have liked to spend Thanksgiving with you. Holidays are for family," she said pointedly.

Alex's smile did not slip. She was wearing her broadcast face. Any emotions she had were hidden behind her broad smile. "It's just my dad. And he is working today so he won't be missing me."

Cane hadn't told his mom anything about Alex. Every time he tried his mom would launch into a tirade about professional ethics and her disdain for journalists in general and Alex Martin in particular.

"Are your parents divorced?" Katrina asked.

"No, mom died when I was six weeks old."

Katrina blinked, clearly not expecting that answer. Cane prayed there would not be a follow-up question but there was. "I'm sorry. How did she die?"

"She committed suicide." Alex did not flinch. She was in full professional mode. Nothing could shake her.

His mom's eyes widened.

Cane reached for Alex's hand and gave it a small squeeze. She glanced at him and smiled.

"I'm sorry," his mother said again.

"That's all right. I never knew her to miss her. And I have my dad. He is great. Maybe you will meet him."

"Yes, that would be nice." Katrina did not manage a smile but the frown that was anchored, lifted slightly.

For a moment silence reigned. "So, are we eating here or at Colt's?" Cane raised an eyebrow.

"Colt's. We can leave as soon as you put your bags away."

Cane waited for his mom to go downstairs before he gathered Alex against him. "You, okay?"

"You weren't kidding when you said your mama doesn't like me." Her eyes rested on the floor like she wanted to fall into the slit between the wooden planks.

Cane let out a stream of air. "She's a mom. You'll be the

same with our kids." Cane kissed her forehead.

A panicked look contorted Alex's features. "Now is not the time to talk about your eleven-pound children."

"Our children," Cane amended. Best she get used to that idea now. "And mama will come round. By the time you have our fourth, you will be BFFs."

"Umm…I doubt that. Come on, Corn Fed. Let's go. Round two of meet the family awaits."

"You already did the hard part. The rest of them will love you. I promise. And even if they don't, I love you." He pulled her in to his chest and kissed her head. Her hair smelled of flowers and vanilla. Cane was hungry for more than the pie she had spent hours trying to perfect.

"I love you, too." Their lips met and something deep inside lit a fire of more than desire. He was not ever going to let go of it.

***

Night Latch was a ten-minute drive from his mom's house. Cheyenne was waiting on the porch, waving, Garron balanced on her hip. Her smile was as bright as her red hair.

"Cheyenne Ford is waving to us," Alex said in amazement. "I can't believe Country's Darling is your sister-in-law." She squeezed his thigh as if he needed to be pinched into reality. The only thing that seemed out of reality for him was Alex. But it was real.

"Wait for it. She is about to hug you. Cheyenne is a hugger."

True to form, as soon as they reached the porch, Cheyenne handed the baby to his mom and reached for Alex. "I am so glad to meet you. I hope you have gotten a proper Texas welcome." Cheyenne gave Cane a knowing look.

"Nice to meet you, too. I have all your albums."

"Do you? Oh, that is so nice. Garron's college fund thanks you."

Alex smiled down at the baby. "He is adorable."

Cheyenne beamed. "I think so. He looks just like Cord and Cane at that age, except he has dark eyes like Colt. Have you met my husband?"

Alex nodded. "Yes, in the helicopter."

Cheyenne laughed. "Of course. He took you to the cottage. Just to warn you, I conceived this guy at the cottage."

Alex coughed.

Cheyenne winked at Cane. Subtle. He would get her back for that later. Cane reached down and scooped up Garron. "Hey, little man. I've missed you. Have you been working on your pass?"

Cheyenne shook her head. "My son is not playing football or competing in a rodeo or choosing a career where animals bite him on a daily basis."

Just then Colt joined them at the front of the house. "We'll see about that. Nice how my wife rules out every career held by a Clayburn man." He leaned over and kissed his wife.

"Not true. He can be a carpenter like your dad. I would like that. Yes, you can build things." The baby giggled as Cheyenne tickled his tummy.

Colt smiled and reached out his hand. "Pleased to officially meet you, Alex."

"Nice to meet you, too."

'So, do you forgive me for stranding you with my brother?" Colt asked.

Alex's cheeks turned a light shade of pink. "The verdict is still out on that one."

"Fair enough. Come on in. Cord just got here. We were just waiting on you. Let's eat."

Cane followed them through to the dining room. Cheyenne had redecorated since he had last been there. His sister-in-law seemed to be systematically putting her stamp on every room. When Colt bought the ranch, he had everything painted white. His brother was a minimalist in every way or at least he had been until he married Cheyenne. Colt was a different man now, happier. He would let Cheyenne paint the house pink if she wanted. He probably wouldn't even notice.

"I like the wall color," Cane said, referring to the burnt orange. "I always knew you were a UT fan at heart. Hook 'Em." Cane held up his hand in the horn sign that represented UT.

Cheyenne shook her head. "I just liked the color. And don't worry Case, I painted the feature wall in the game room maroon."

Case smiled. "Gig 'Em…that's the best place in the house where things get settled." He pretended to break a stick with two hands. "Saw 'em off." His brother laughed.

"Alex, the Aggie over here is my brother Case."

"The nice one. That is how he describes you, by the way." Alex reached out her hand to shake but Case wrapped his arms around her in an embrace.

"I would actually say Case is the handsome one, but yeah he is the nicest, too." Jamison stood and hugged Alex. "I'm Jamison. Pleasure to meet you. And welcome to this interesting family."

"Clearly. I am the handsome one." Cord rounded the corner.

Alex looked from Cord to Cane and back again. Her eyes widened. "You look more like twins than brothers."

"Look closer, I'm better looking," Cord said as he hugged Alex.

Alex squinted. "Oh yes, I see it. You're right. Sorry, Cane. Cord is the cute one."

Everyone laughed, except Cane. Alex would be paying for that one later. God, he wanted to kiss her. But if he kissed her, he would want more. His eyes cut to the table. "Three turkeys. Nice. PETA is going to take away your vegan card, Cheyenne."

Cheyenne rolled her eyes. "That happened when I married the cowboy. Seems my ethics were thoroughly compromised by this one."

"Darlin, I compromised you but it had nothing to do with meat." Colt pulled Cheyenne and kissed her temple.

"And yes, three turkeys. I am not having the annual drumstick war on my watch. There is enough for every Clayburn to have one."

Jamison cleared his throat.

"And yes. I can't forget you, J."

"Colt, can you say grace so we can start. Garron is not going to last much longer. We are on borrowed time as it is. Your son was scheduled for a tantrum fifteen minutes ago. He just dropped his afternoon nap," Cheyenne explained. "Which is a bummer because those were my favorite ninety minutes of the day." She let out a sigh.

"Yeah, they were." Colt shot Cheyenne a knowing glance and she smiled and shook her head.

"Alex, you are sitting down here by me. And Katrina, you are sitting down at the bottom by Jamison." Cheyenne caught Cane's eye. True to her word Cheyenne had separated Alex and his mom.

Everyone took their seats and then Colt said Grace.

"Wow, this all looks so good," Alex said. "I have never seen so much food at one dinner table."

"And it will all be gone in twenty minutes. The Clayburns don't do leftovers." Cheyenne laughed.

Katrina nodded. "Tell me about it. We really don't. I thought you boys would bankrupt us."

"You think this is a lot of food, wait for Christmas. It's all this plus roast beef," Cord said.

"Wow," Alex said. "Christmas for my dad and I is always Chinese." She seemed to realize what she had just said. "Neither of us cook. So…it's always Nine Dragons." Alex looked down at the mashed potatoes that had just been passed to her. She took a spoonful and then passed them to Cheyenne who was trying unsuccessfully to distract the baby. Garron whined and arched his back. Alex scooped some potatoes onto Cheyenne's plate for her and passed the bowl to Colt.

"Your timing is not great, baby boy," Cheyenne said as she stood up with him. "I need to walk him. Clayburn boys like to be on the move."

"Do you want me to take him? It's the least I could do after you prepared this entire meal," Alex offered.

Cane caught her eye. She was scared. He had never seen her like this. The reporter exterior was gone and what was left was ready to bolt out the door.

"No, you eat." Cheyenne waved for her to sit down.

"Okay, I think I'll just step outside for a moment. I think I need to get some air."

Cane caught Cheyenne's eye and nodded. Thankfully she understood. "You know what, that would be great if you walked him. I'm exhausted and hungry." Cheyenne handed Garron to Alex.

Alex blinked like she wasn't expecting Cheyenne to hand her the baby.

"Oh, hello little guy. I'm Alex."

"Do you want me to come with you?" Cane offered softly.

"Oh, no. Stay and enjoy the meal."

Alex carried Garron outside. Cane turned to look at his family who were all staring at him. For a long time, no one spoke. Jamison was the first to break the silence. "I like her. I like her a lot. I think we might have been too much for her."

"You guys are too much for me and I've known you my entire life," Cheyenne said as she swallowed a mouthful of green beans. She was taking full advantage of not having a baby on her lap, to enjoy her meal.

"She is not used to so many people. It's always just been her and her dad," Cane explained, hoping that is what it was.

"What did you do to her?" Katrina asked, her voice stern.

Everyone turned to look at her. Her arms were crossed over her chest. She was wearing the same look she did the day he broke the stained-glass window at church with his slingshot.

"I love you, son. I love all my boys. You know that. But you can't pull the wool over my eyes." She pressed her lips together as if it were an attempt to hold back further words.

"What?"

"Those articles were payback for something. I can see that now. That woman loves you but you hurt her. So, answer the question; what did you do to her?"

Cane shook his head. "I only met her after she wrote the first article. I've never done anything to her," he said incredulously.

"Nope." She was unconvinced. "I know people. I was all prepared to really not like that girl but then I saw her with you and it is clear she loves you. So, answer the question. What did you do? Did you sleep with her roommate and not call? Did you say something to upset her? Did you insult her daddy? What did you do to that girl?" His mama's gaze bore down on him.

Cane pulled at his collar. Damn, it was hot in here. "Mama, I only met the woman at the start of the season. I have not had time to do any of those things." He tried to make a joke to diffuse the situation but Katrina was having none of it.

"Hmm. You did something. I suggest you figure it out and apologize."

"Somebody just got sacked." Cord tsked before he tore a drumstick off the turkey closest to him.

"I can still whip your ass," Cane warned him.

"I would like to see you try." Cord's mouth pulled up into a lazy smile.

"Can you save it until after dessert," Cheyenne asked. "I want to enjoy my dinner. But if we are taking bets, my money is on Cane. Sorry Cord, he has fifty pounds on you."

"I don't know," Colt interjected. "Cord has always been scrappy. He might surprise you."

"Yep, my money is on Cord, too," Case said.

"I'm with Cheyenne on this one," Jamison chimed in.

"You always take Cheyenne's side," Cord said. "She could say that Garron was the starting tight end for the Cowboys and you would nod your head like a puppy."

"Over my dead body is my son playing for the Cowboys." Cheyenne did not bother swallowing.

"What she said," Colt agreed.

His family continued to eat, talk and laugh. It was good to have everyone in the same place at one time. It didn't happen very often anymore. They were all too busy with their own lives. Eventually Colt stood to clear the dishes. Alex and Garron had been gone for the better part of an hour but Cheyenne didn't seem to mind. She was too busy full of laughter and almost tears of happiness with Case and Jamison to notice. Cane walked through the large house in search of Alex. Eventually he found her in the study on the couch. Garron was asleep soundly on her shoulder. Cane stood in the doorway and took in the scene. Pride and love swelled in his chest. Alex was going to be a good mama. She didn't know it yet but she would be amazing. She would throw herself into it the way she threw herself into everything else. She would be great. Their kids would be lucky.

"Hey," he called softly. "I saved you a plate."

Alex surprised him by saying, "Thank you. I'm starving."

"Do you want me to take Garron so you can go eat?"

"Not yet. Smell his head. He smells so sweet. Who knew babies smelled this good?"

Cane smiled down at them. "I thought you weren't a fan of kids."

"I'm not in general but this one is pretty great. And look at his chubby little fingers. Have you ever seen anything this precious?"

"Yeah. Yeah, I have." He smiled down at her.

Alex smiled back. She lowered her voice to a whisper. "So, when you mentioned earlier that I wouldn't be Case's type was that because despite my awesomeness…I don't have the right parts?" Her nose scrunched up and Cane wanted to kiss it. Cane laughed. "You mean is he gay? I hope so because his boyfriend is and it would be really awkward for them if he wasn't."

"Jamison is his partner?" She tapped her lips as if she had put two and two together.

"Yes. Cord is the only Clayburn on the market. So, if you have any single friends."

"I'm sure Cord does just fine on his own."

Cane's smile slipped. "What's this about him being the handsome brother?"

"Nope that's you, Cane. And you're the nice one, too. But don't tell anyone that. You got to give them something."

"And I'm the smart one, too?"

"Don't push it, Corn Fed."

Cane leaned down and kissed Alex's forehead. The baby stirred between them.

"Shh, it's okay baby," Alex soothed. Garron stretched then settled back against her shoulder. Cane took out his phone and snapped a picture of Alex and the baby.

"You better not put that on Twitter. Your fangirls already throw me enough shade. If I have to read another 'why is he with her' comment I will start blocking people. Like all female people."

"I'm with you cause I love you. And cause you stopped running long enough for me to catch you."

"I thought you were with me because I teach you the big words and because I'm probably the only woman that understands football more than you." She raised an eyebrow at him.

"Only because of the thesaurus I bought you and you do not know football more than me." He tugged on her hair. "But it is a perk and there are other perks I can't talk about in front of the baby. But mostly it's just because I love you."

"Oh, there ya'll are," Cheyenne called as she rounded the corner. "Ah, bless him, he was so tired from playing with his uncles." Cheyenne picked up Garron and kissed him. The baby slept through it; blissfully unaware he had changed arms. "I'll see y'all in the dining room. Katrina said the pecan pie is vegan. You're now officially my favorite sister-in-law. That was so sweet of you and thanks for holding my little man." She patted his back. "It was bliss to eat a meal with a knife and fork. You can come over anytime you want." Cheyenne flickered her lashes at Cane. "Bring her back, Cane. I like her. And so does Garron."

Cheyenne headed back toward the kitchen.

"You, okay?" Cane made sure Cheyenne was out of earshot.

Alex nodded. "I'm good." Her broadcaster smile was plastered on her face. The one that hid everything. How long would it take her to lower the mask to be around his family?

"You're not, sweetheart. I can tell." Cane paused for a second wondering if he should bring up what his mama said at dinner. It made sense that Alex had an ax to grind. She had never slighted another player like that before or since. Looking at it now, it definitely seemed personal.

"Listen…um…about my mama. She seems to think I did something to upset you to make you write those articles."

Alex froze, her body went rigid, but her face was still impassive. "I just want to forget those articles. I wish I had never written them."

Cane tilted her chin up so she was looking him in the eye. "I don't. I'm grateful every day for those articles. I would never have met you if it weren't for them."

Alex's eyes went dark, almost vacant, like she was looking through him. Her smile slipped.

"What is it, Alex. What is it you're not telling me? Did I upset you? Was it my mama?"

"No. She is fine. They're all fine. They're great. It's just too much. I have no idea how to be part of that dynamic. I know how to be a daughter. I know how to be a friend. I know how to be a reporter. I know how to do those things. I don't know how to do this."

"You know how to be a great girlfriend. Don't forget to add that to your list."

Alex rolled her eyes. "Ha! You only think that cause I'm your first. Trust me, Corn Fed, I'm not."

Cane took her hands in his. "You're perfect for me. That's all that matters. You've broken me for other women."

Alex shook her head. "Don't put that on Twitter, either. Texan fans will be leaving horse heads in my bed."

Cane leaned down and kissed her. He kept it brief because he knew if he kissed her for any length of time, he would need to have her. "Let's go have dessert before my brothers eat it all."

"Seriously how did your parents afford to feed you all?"

Cane took Alex's hand and led her back to the dining room. "Clayburn men always find a way."

His mama smiled at them. "There you are. We just started dessert. Alex this is the best pecan pie I have ever had. I need this recipe."

Alex glanced up at Cane, bewilderment in her eyes, clearly not expecting the about face in his mom. "Oh...sure. I will send it to you."

"Or you can make it for me next time I'm in Houston. I haven't been to a game all season. I should do that." Katrina nodded her head as if she had made a final decision.

Bewilderment turned to shock. Alex's mouth dropped open. For a moment, Alex didn't say anything. Cane gave her hand a small squeeze. "Oh...wow. That would be nice. I could make dinner after the December home game. I think you're playing the Chiefs. I mean, if you're playing again by then."

"Oh, I will be back by then." Cane took in more than a mouthful of pie and swallowed it without a single chew. He didn't need anything to help settle his stomach. He was ready to be back in the game and Alex in his arms.

***

Of course, his mama put Alex in Colt's room. It meant he had to walk past her room to get there, across the squeakiest floorboards in Texas. Cane waited as long as he could after his mom went to bed to make his move. Cord was still downstairs but Cane did not have the patience for his brother to go to bed, too. Given brother code, he didn't have to worry about Cord. It was only that damn wooden board. Like a trip wire of mine fields. Cane's memory held as he made his way across the floor without the slightest of squeaks.

Alex's eyes widened when he opened the door. She was cross legged on top of the covers with her pen in hand as she scribbled something in her notebook. Alex was always writing something down, probably for a story.

"What are you doing?" Alex dropped her pen on the bed.

Cane shrugged his shoulders and smiled. "It seems pretty obvious. I am going to figuratively sleep with you and then literally sleep with you. I miss you, Alex. I didn't sleep with you last night, either. That's not acceptable. If we're in the same city, you're in my bed. Or Colt's bed as the case may be. My high school self is high fiving me right now. I am about to sleep with a beautiful woman in my big brother's bed." Pride filled his lungs.

Alex shook her head. "You are ridiculous." Her head might have shaken side to side but her eyes were in full request for a touchdown in the bed mode.

"So you keep telling me. But you're wearing my jersey. You know what that does to me. I can't not fuck you when you wear that. It's impossible."

Alex held up her hand to stop him from getting any closer. "You will not fit in this bed. You are literally bigger than a twin mattress."

"I'll fit. I'm used to putting big things into small spaces."

"So ridiculous. I'm serious, Cane. Even if you fit on this bed, there would be no room for me."

"Umm…on top of me. You're feeding me the lines tonight."

Alex paused like she needed to consider it but then shook her head. "No. I just got your mom on my side. I'm not going to ruin it by defiling her son in her home. Go to bed, Corn Fed."

"My mom knows you have defiled me already. So, you might as well do it again, sweetheart."

"I'm serious. We will wake up your mom."

"No, we won't. We'll pretend we're in high school. And we have to be quiet so we don't get caught. God, I wish I would have met you in high school."

Alex scrunched her nose. "No, you don't. I hadn't discovered straighteners and I had a retainer. It wasn't pretty."

"Yep, I wish we would have met in high school. I would have spent all four years trying to get into your pants."

"You wouldn't have had to try that hard, Corn Fed. I think we've established I have a hard time resisting you."

"I'm serious. Look at all the time we've wasted. I was All State. You should have written a scathing article about me then. I would have tracked you down."

Alex shook her head. "Go to bed, Corn Fed. I love you but this is not happening."

"Woman we are going to have sex. Whether we wake up the house is up to you. I can be quiet when I come. Can you?" he challenged.

"I know you dare me to do things just to get your own way."

"And yet, you still do them."

Alex reached her hand out for him. "We already established I find you very hard to resist."

"Then stop trying." Cane lowered them both to the bed, the frame squeaked under the weight.

"We're going to break the bed," Alex whispered against

his mouth. With each syllable her lips caressed his. Instantly he was hard.

"I'll buy a new one."

"Not the point." Alex smiled.

"Woman, what part of we're having sex didn't you understand?"

Alex groaned.

"See, if you make those noises someone will hear us."

"I'm not the one who is going to get us caught," she whispered. "If we're going to do this you need to get on your back."

"If you want to ride me, sweetheart, just ask. You don't need to make excuses."

"Did anyone ever tell you, you're very cocky?"

"You do most days and yet here we are." Cane stood up to let Alex move from underneath him. He stripped his boxers off.

Alex smiled at him appreciatively. "To be fair, you have a lot to be cocky about." This time it was Alex who pushed Cane down against the bed. She pulled the jersey over her head and dropped it to the ground. "If we're going to do this, it's my rules, Corn Fed."

"Oh, we're doing it." Cane tried to pull Alex down but she wriggled away.

"First rule." Alex grabbed his hands and pushed them above his head then wrapped them around the wrought iron spindles of the headboard. "No touching. You let go, and I'm sending you back to your room. You'll be getting no high fives from your high-school-self tonight."

"But you like when I touch you." Cane licked his lips. She liked when he used his tongue to touch her as well. He was sure of that.

"Second rule: You make a sound and we stop. Any sound. Do you accept my rules?"

"Sweetheart, if it means I get to be inside you, I accept." God he would accept anything from her. Anything.

CHAPTER NINETEEN

And then it happened. It. The call. The call of her life. The one Alex had daydreamed about since she was a little girl and decided that since she couldn't play on the field, she would report about it. She loved to write and talk to people, get them to divulge more than they had wanted to share. Sometimes it was awkward but it was pure and authentic and everyone was closer because of it. Most times. There were a few instances of a disclosure that made someone uncomfortable but that was an emotion and that was what Alex needed and strived to make happen.

Emotions were what made the story that much more powerful. The tears that glistened in the parents' eyes as they talked about the first time their child picked up a bat or ball. The tears of sadness that trickled down a players' face as they watched the last chance to make the playoffs dissipate before them. Dreams vanished and dreams achieved. Each story with the climax of a triumph or defeat.

The only emotion Alex had right now was anticipation of success. Finally. It happened she had superseded her own goals. She had surpassed all her dreams. Alex had wanted to be an on-air sideline reporter and it happened. But now she was going to be an on-air anchor for ESPN. She shook her head and ran around the room. The details would be in route to her email but the basics had already been disclosed. Connecticut was to be her new home.

And then the lump of fear pulled up into the back of her throat. Not once as they spoke had she considered the idea of Houston not being her home base. If she was in Connecticut, that would not work for her and Cane. Even if they tried it wouldn't. It was too far. With their combined schedules it was already a challenge but throw in a different home base and it wasn't even the same game. It would be two different worlds. Worlds that wouldn't meet. It wouldn't work. All the excitement that had raced through her veins and made her lungs pump harder was gone. It had sunk into a spot of reality.

Run the reel again. The real reel. The one that points out all the ways it doesn't make sense and how it would be over. Her lungs constricted until she couldn't breathe. It hurt. Alex couldn't breathe at all. This was the worst. She was in the crux of two things. Not things. One incredible opportunity and the love of her life. Yes, Cane was the love of her life. He always had been. And even with the redo she couldn't see them with a happy ever after as being the last words in their book. No. God. Why? Why couldn't she have it all? She shook her head. Alex let out a deep breath.

She hit her dad's number. Maybe he could provide some form of advice or guidance. Alex never reached out to him for matters of the heart, but maybe this time it would make sense.

"Alexandra, this call is unexpected."

Of course, it was unexpected. She just called to chat and to hopefully get some words of wisdom, but it wasn't a Sunday or Monday and those were the only days they spoke because those were football days, and that is what they talked about. That was their language.

"Yes, I have some exciting news. ESPN has offered me an anchor spot." The thrill she had experienced earlier rose and made her blood tingle.

"That's wonderful, Alexandra. I'm proud of you. You have never taken the short cuts or handouts. This is all you. Your mother would be so excited for you." His voice choked at the mention of her mother. He never spoke of her. *Ever.*

Alex swallowed. It took her a second to be able to speak. "Thank you. I'm just a little on edge…I don't…I…what do you think about Cane?"

"Cane is definitely one of the best quarterbacks in the league. I'm glad to see him back on the field. The hit he took against The Patriots, I would have thought he was out for the season. But he's back and looking solid."

Her lips twisted in unison with her heart. There was nothing left to ask or say. Her dad wasn't going there. He wouldn't. This was not the relationship they had. Theirs was different from other families. They talked football not feelings. This was okay. Alex would solve this situation on her own as she had so many other things.

"Yea, he's great. Alright, well I've got to go and figure all of this out."

"You do that, Alexandra. I love you."

"I love you, too." She hit the end button and slunk down into her couch. The couch where Cane had delivered orgasms and emotions. Levels she had never reached but with him she did. Everything she did was better and different with him. Could she give this up? Could Alex give up Cane? He wouldn't want to be together if she took the job. She was sure of that.

Her phone buzzed. She ignored it. Alex couldn't handle another phone call or even a text. She was alone in a world of uncertainty. Too many *what ifs* dangled in the air and she had nothing to grab onto. Cane. She wanted him. But he was an uncertainty, too. He was a risk. The position in Connecticut wasn't. It was a solid. If she did her job right, and she would, it was hers and no one could take it away from her. But with Cane it wasn't up to only her. It was him and them together. The doubt and previous fears swarmed through her mind and it overwhelmed Alex. The idea of them being a couple seemed less and less of a reality and more and more of a happenstance, like fairytale that would never come to fruition and have its own happily-ever-after. No, it was most likely over.

Her phone buzzed again. It was Vanessa. Alex hit the green button. "Hey."

"Hey! I saw the announcement from your office online. Hellooo!" Vanessa shrieked into the phone.

"I know. It's incredible….but…" Alex sighed. She was so confused. This was the moment in her dream she never thought would happen. Confliction and unanticipated heartache pulsed through her body like a freight train about to go off the tracks.

"But what? What's the problem? What happened? Do they want you to dye your hair blond or something?" Vanessa laughed. "Tell me that isn't it. Tell me they don't want you to be like some sort of Fox-snoozes Fembot." Vanessa paused as if the phone connection had been lost.

Alex was silent.

"Hello Alex, are you there, that's not it is it?" Vanessa demanded.

"No, it's I just, I want it…its' really exciting but it means…well…you know…" Alex pulled on the threads of her blanket. She wanted to unravel them the way the strings that had wrapped up her heart were now coming undone.

"What do I know?" Vanessa sighed. "Is this about him? Tell me you are not going to risk your career and future on another Fake Blitz from Cane Clayburn."

Alex rolled back her shoulders. "No, I'm not. I'm okay. Let's get drinks on Thursday."

"Definitely, we are going to celebrate! Rosie's it is."

Alex hung up the phone. She glanced at the time. He would be there any time now. Suddenly, she heard the sound of knocking at her door. Her body stiffened. *It's now or never.*

Alex had known about the job, her move, and the end of their relationship for a week and not once had she mentioned it to Cane. She'd allowed it to sit in the back of her mind never allowing herself to acknowledge it while she was with him. Today would be different, though. Today, she would tell him and that would be it. The insides of her heart concaved at the idea but it had to be done. The position had been taken and her lease had been terminated. She paused for a second at the door. No, she couldn't leave him outside. She had to let him in.

"You, okay?" Cane raised an eyebrow at her as she pulled the door open.

Alex forced a smile on her face. "I'm always, okay," she lied. Cane needed to think she was okay and that she would be okay without him. It would make it easier for both of them.

"Are you sure?" He gathered her into his arms and his lips pressed against her forehead. "You'd tell me if something was wrong, wouldn't you?"

Alex froze. No, she wouldn't. She hadn't. This day would not end well, that was a guarantee.

"Of course." Two lies. Alex bit the inside of her cheek. Not good. At no point did she ever want to lie to Cane. Technically, she hadn't until now.

"Hmm…alright, well are you ready?" Cane's brow furrowed.

"Ready, I thought we were going to spend the day in bed?" This was how she wanted to spend their last day together. All of him to herself. One last time.

The sides of his lips pulled up. "Alex, if I hadn't seen your lady parts I would be convinced you were a man with the amount of sex you are always asking for."

"I wasn't exactly, asking. I think it was more of a demand and I want it delivered now." She poked his chest.

He grabbed her finger. "We'll have time for that later, but right now we have got to get on the road." Cane's eyes scanned her body and stopped on her feet. She had on three-inch red heels with little slits that ran along the sides. Alex had bought them as a treat to herself for the big promotion. Now, they were more of a resemblance of what was to come. A broken heart.

"Do you have a pair of flats?"

"Flats? Has your ego taken a bruising and you need to be more than a foot taller than me?" She pursed her lips together.

Cane laughed. "Sweetheart, you could be in stilts and my ego would be just as big." He leaned down and captured her lips then her tongue and her heart came undone. He did that to her. Every time. This would be more than difficult. Cane pulled away. "But my ego is only overinflated because I've got you at my side." He swatted her behind. "Now, go grab some different shoes."

Alex made her way to the closet and considered the idea of climbing in, rocking back and forth and not delivering the decision that had been made to Cane. She grabbed her brown ballerina slippers. They resembled a freshly created mud puddle, the kind with a tiny amount of reflection where you can almost see yourself. Good thing she couldn't really see her reflection because hers was one of despair and a shattered heart. It had not even been officially broken yet, but it was coming and the anticipation hurt just the same.

"So where are we going?" Alex glanced out the window. The sun had lowered into a sweet pink haze on the horizon. Down it went, further behind the clouds before it completely disappeared.

"A pretty view. Not as gorgeous as the one I'm looking at right now but I think you will like it." He winked at her.

Her chest squeezed tight. Oxygen was on a drought in her lungs. The longer she withheld on the discussion the less likely she would be able to find the strength to speak the words that needed to be said.

"We've been driving for over an hour. And not in the direction of Cut and Shoot so where are we going, Corn

Fed?" Alex was confused as to the destination of this drive. If he had wanted to show her Christmas lights, they wouldn't have needed to leave the city limits of Houston. The displays were on record as being one of the best cities in the world.

"Why don't you find us a good song?" He nodded toward the stereo.

"Fine and then you tell me where we are going." She rubbed her lips together and scanned through the stations.

"Run your spur along me all day." Played over the speaker. Alex let a small smile form on her lips.

"Anything but that." Cane tried to move her fingers.

"Where are we going?" Alex moved her head in front of the button to block his attempt.

"Tie me up in your lies."

Cane's nostrils flared and he pressed his lips together.

"Wrap me up in your rope."

"Austin, we are going to Austin. Are you happy?"

"Boot deep happy." Alex laughed. She knew his weaknesses. He loved Cheyenne with all his heart but to listen to her sing a song she had obviously written about having sex with his brother was too much for him. It was his breaking point.

But why were they in route to Austin? Did he finally figure it out? Had he known all along and had played her or made her think he didn't? Alex swallowed. If he knew, if he really knew and this was his way of saying sorry and to ask for forgiveness, could she do it? Could she still follow through and leave? Would she? The questions rolled through her mind until they began to coast around the curves of Mt Bonnell Road. Alex's breath escaped her lungs and fear raced around her. He knew. He was going to apologize. He was going to make it better. All those tears were going to be placed in a bucket and dumped into Lake Austin. They would be left there. He wanted her. He was going to fix what had been broken. Alex would not be able to leave him, not after that. No.

She rubbed her lips together.

"Have you been here before?" Cane squeezed her leg. She jumped. "With someone else?"

"No." No. Alex had never gone to Mount Bonnell. Neither of them had, unless he had come after that night. They had laughed about it. How everyone had raved about it and how beautiful the view was and they made the decision to go together. To write off this Austin bucket list item.

Cane reached for her hand and kissed her on the head as they took the first step of the next one hundred and six that would follow. Side by side they rose to the next level. The hill was steep. With each stair, each stone Alex left behind all of her fears and concerns about Cane. This was it. He was the one. They could do this. No matter what they were in it together. This was possible. It wasn't a happenstance fairytale. This was real. He was real. They were real and so right for each other. He was going to make it right. Alex's stomach clenched into a tiny ball of hope.

The view was better than anyone had ever described. Even a picture wouldn't be able to capture this incredible display. Lights scattered along the shores of the lakes and further in the distance, were like tiny sparkles of opportunity in the darkness. They reminded her of a missed moment that hadn't happened back then, but now was going to come into fruition. This was it.

Cane glanced at the lake and back to Alex. "Alex, I've finally met the only woman in the world that can match me on each play of the game of life and I've brought you up here to the highest point in Austin. I wish we would have met in college and I would have done this sooner." He began to bend at the knee.

"No, stop. Don't take a knee. You said you only wanted to do that once, right?"

"Right." His eyes widened.

"Well, you haven't met me once." Her lungs were squeezed so hard the air had evacuated her body. With all her might she blurted out., "We knew each other in college."

"What?" He shook his head. His brows furrowed in confusion.

Alex took a step back. "You really don't remember, do you?"

He ran his fingers through his hair and stood in silence.

"We were in a study group together. Business 101." She paused. Nothing. No flash of a memory reflected in his eyes. "You came over to my house and no studying took place. You were really flirty and I had been crushing on you. Well, more than crushing on you all semester and we made out. Does any of this sound familiar to you?" Despite the lack of air, the blood in her veins began to pulsate as if in an attempt to perform CPR on her. A small panic attack raced underneath her skin. Beads of sweat trickled against the back of her hair.

"No."

Alex tapped the sides of her head. She forced herself to tame the flames that ran inside her. She could do this. She inhaled. "Let me continue. We had a great time or at least I thought we did. We made plans to watch Legends of the Fall and then go take a guess Cane. I think you might have enough smarts to figure this one out?" Her cheeks were on fire. Anger and humiliation burned in her. A welt of pain seared against her skin as it resurfaced from so many years ago.

"Here?"

"Yes, here. Neither of us had been here at the time. Though, now I'm guessing you took lots of women here. This must be your thing. You must do it so much that you can't even remember it. Just like me." Alex pushed a rock on the ground toward the edge. She pressed her eyes shut. This had to be a nightmare. Not her life.

"Alex, let me explain. Business 101?"

"Yes."

"My dad died that semester."

Chills ran against her arms.

"Yes, I went through a lot of women and a lot of booze. So, I'm sorry that I fucked up. If I had not been doing that, I guarantee you, I would have remembered."

Alex shook her head. "Well, you didn't remember then, either. I showed up at your room the next day with the picnic we had agreed upon and you had no clue who I was or why I was there. Do you know what that feels like?" She couldn't breathe. Instantly she was transported back in time, the wounds fresh. Oh god, it hurt…the humiliation.

"No."

"Well, it's awful. Like let me drop sixty pounds of shame awful. That's right, I weighed sixty pounds more back then, so I can thank you for that. I'm eighty pounds lighter now. But who's counting?" She laughed. It was fake. Not real. Just like them.

"I am and I'm sorry." Cane reached for her hands but she pulled away.

Alex swallowed. "It's too late for sorry. I can't do this and neither can you. We weren't meant to be. Let's leave it as a good time and no regrets." She stepped back. She needed to create physical distance from him. Any closer and he could pull her in and it would be too hard to let go.

"Are you serious? Because I fucked up six years ago you are ending everything we have now?"

"No, I'm ending everything now because I'm moving. I've taken a job in Connecticut I'm going to be an anchor. I was going to tell you today." She swallowed hard. She let pride fill her lungs as if she could pretend that her pride for her job was more important than the idea of them.

"What?"

"Now, I'm the one that's sorry. I should have told you earlier. But I just couldn't." Alex glanced down. She needed to get out of here. Off this mountain that was bigger than a molehill and get back to Houston. Time to end the day. Everything else was already over.

"How long have you known?"

Alex forced herself to make eye contact. "A week."

"Alex, you've known for a week and you weren't going to tell me? Until today? Why?" He stepped toward her. His eyes were light as they reflected the moon.

"Because, I wanted to have one last week with you." She rubbed her lips together and bit the inside of her cheek. *Do not cry. Get out.*

"You didn't want us to end. That's why you didn't say anything. Don't lie to yourself." Cane reached for her hand again but she pulled away.

"I'm not. I have to go. My flight leaves tomorrow." Alex turned on her heel and thanked herself for the ballet shoes. They got her off the hill faster than what would seem possible. She ran as quickly as her feet would allow and then found a spot to crouch down and hide. It was dark. No one would see the tear that had escaped her eye. She retrieved her phone from her purse and texted Vanessa.

"Please pick me up. I'm at the bottom of Mount Bonnell."

Vanessa would know what this meant. She knew what Mount Bonnell was to Alex. The mountain she would never climb. It was always out of her reach, just like Cane.

CHAPTER TWENTY

Fuck. Where was she? He shouldn't have let her run, it was dark. She shouldn't be alone. This was not how this day was supposed to go. Cane wished he really did have a time machine. Not just for today but for back then. Shit. He had really effed up. He knew his drinking had gotten out of hand but he didn't care back then. He just wanted to drink until the pain was numb. He took the rest of it out on the field. Cane ran his hand through his hair and pressed up against a tree. At the bottom of the hill, he spotted her. She was hunched into a ball with her arms crossed tight across her chest. So small and vulnerable in the dark woods. And the biggest threat to her was him. The pain of this tore him up inside. He made his way toward her. He could fix this. He had to. When Alex saw him, she tried to walk away but he caught her and held her tight against him.

"Don't. Don't run, Alex. We can fix this."

Alex went rigid against him. "Cane, if you ever really cared about me, you will let me go right now. I can't. I can't do this right now. I just need…" Her voice cracked.

Shit, please don't cry. He had never seen Alex cry. She didn't cry. She was Alex, his strong capable Alex. Oh fuck! He had made her cry. The realization was a blow to the chest. He had to fix this. "Alex, please—"

"My friend is coming to pick me up. I'll call you tomorrow." She pulled away from him but he wasn't going to let go. Not now. Never.

"I'm not going to leave you here alone."

"Please." Alex's voice was barely a whisper. He had to strain to hear her. "Please, Cane. I need to be alone tonight. I'll speak to you tomorrow."

"You're shaking." Cane took off his coat and wrapped it around her shoulders. "Let me take you home."

Alex shook her head. "Vanessa is coming for me. She is picking me up at Mozart's. I'm fine. Please, Cane. Please leave me alone. I can't talk about this now." A tear slid down her cheek.

"Alex," he pleaded. "Please. Please let me in." He kissed her cheek.

Alex wiped her eyes with the back of her hand. "Do you love me?" Her voice was strong again.

Cane nodded. "Of course. More than I have ever loved anyone else. I love you. I want to marry you and have babies and—"

"If you love me, you'll leave right now. I'm going to sit in Mozart's and wait for Vanessa. I'm fine. Or will be once I am alone. I can't be around you right now."

He didn't want to let her go. Every cell in his body commanded him to hold on to her and not let go. But he couldn't. She asked him for space. And he would give it to her, tonight, only tonight. Then they would fix this. They could fix it. They had to. Cane could not imagine a future without Alex in it. He would fix this. "Promise me you will call as soon as you get home."

Alex nodded.

"No, promise. Say the words, Alex."

"I promise."

Cane followed her to Mozart's but he didn't go in. Alex asked for space and he would give it to her. Cane sat in the parking lot and watched her through the picture window as she drank cup after cup of coffee. Two hours later, Alex left, her best friend by her side. Cane had never met Vanessa but he recognized the short brunette from the picture on Alex's desk. Cane didn't start his car. Even after she had left, he sat, thinking. Had he met Alex before? No. It wasn't possible. He would remember her. They had a connection. He felt it immediately. In the locker room they sparked. It was intense and instant. And then in her office, as soon as he kissed her…no, he would remember her. He pinched the bridge of his nose between his thumb and forefinger. He played back every conversation they had had since they'd met. Fuck. She had given him clues. All the times he thought there was something off…shit, even his mama could see it. Why? Why couldn't he remember her? Cane shook his head. He knew the answer but he didn't want to admit it. Fuck. Cane grasped the steering wheel until his knuckles turned white. There had been a lot of women that year, more than he could count. If he wasn't on the field, he was getting drunk or sleeping around. That is what he did, how he coped. He had hardly been a saint before his dad died, but after, he'd crumbled. He wasn't proud of the way he behaved. He had been an ass, a complete fucking moron.

But how? How could he not remember Alex? And why? Why not tell him? She had so many opportunities. At Thanksgiving he asked her point blank if they had met before and she didn't say anything. Would she have ever told him if he hadn't taken her to Mt Bonnell? She thought he took lots of women there. Never. He had never been to the top. Four years of college and he had never done it. He had thought about it plenty of times but never got round to doing it, not until tonight. He wanted to propose to Alex there because…God, he didn't even know why he wanted to do it there. Something in the back of his mind told him that should be the spot because they had both gone to UT and yet their paths had never crossed. Shit. He had really fucked up. He needed to go home. He had practice in the morning. But he didn't want to go home to an empty house.

He was supposed to be taking Alex home to their house, where they would live and bring home their babies and raise a family. This is not how tonight was supposed to go.

Cane's phone vibrated: A message from Alex. "*I'm home.*"

Shit how long had he been sitting in his car? It was past midnight. Cane dialed Alex's number but it went to voicemail.

"Call me back, Alex. I love you. I don't care what time you get this, just call."

***

Cane paused before he dialed Alex's number. This was the last time, the last call. He loved her but it was clear it was over. She'd lied when she said she would call him the next day. She never called, texted, emailed or sent a smoke signal or any of the other fucking ways she could have contacted him.

It was over. Alex made that clear. He never pegged her for a god-dammed coward. Yeah, she didn't like confrontation, but this was ridiculous. He had fucked up six years ago, but their relationship was *now*. They had fallen in love now. And if she was willing to give that up because of a stupid mistake…then he was done, too.

Cane held his breath when he pushed call. Almost immediately the call went to voicemail. He let out a bitter laugh. Well, there it was. Over, as quickly as it had started. *Really, on Christmas Eve, you send me to voicemail.*

Cane put his phone back in his pocket. He was already late. He should have left for Cut and Shoot an hour ago. He was dragging his feet because he was stupid enough to think that he would get ahold of Alex and everything would somehow be okay. He hadn't told his family they had broken up, because he didn't want to believe that they had. That was going to be a fun conversation with his mother, telling her that she was right, and he was indeed an asshole and had ruined things with the only woman he had ever loved. Cane shook his head. There was no point in putting it off or making excuses, it was what it was. They had fun for a while but now it was over. Cane loaded the trunk with the presents he was taking home to his family. He smiled when he saw the tiny football for Garron. The boy had good hands; he could already see it. He had quarterback written all over him. Cheyenne would fight it, but that was happening. This was Texas. The boy would play football. Cane tossed the ball on top of the other gifts then stopped cold when he saw the unwrapped gift he had bought for Alex. He had forgotten about it. He saw it in a shop at the airport and gotten it for her. Cane held up the burnt orange UT baby onesie. On the front there was a longhorn with the word *Texas* curved above it. He bought it for their baby. The one they were going to have someday, the one he had been joking about since he met Alex. But it wasn't a joke for him. Cane wanted that life with Alex.

Shit, he still wanted it. He still wanted her. He always would. Damn it. Cane sighed. He had called and texted Alex a hundred times since they broke up. She wasn't talking to him. He had no way of finding her, short of going to the ESPN studio in Connecticut and making a complete ass of himself. Not that he was above that, he just had no idea if she would be there, either. She could be reporting from anywhere. All he knew is that she wasn't at Texans games or practices. He had looked. Every time he was at the stadium, he hoped he would see her, but he never did.

It was nearly six o' clock on Christmas Eve, Cane knew where Alex was today. This was the one day of the year he could be sure. She was in Oklahoma with her dad. Cane was supposed to be there, too. That is how it was supposed to be. Fuck it. He wasn't done calling her or chasing her or loving her. He wasn't going to be done with that until…ever. He would never be over her.

He needed to get to the airport. He would call his mama from there and tell her he wasn't coming home this year. He needed to bring Alex back. His hands were slick. Shit, he was nervous. Cane looked at the board. There was one flight to Oklahoma but not until 9 o'clock, by the time he rented a car, he wouldn't be there until almost midnight.

CHAPTER TWENTY-ONE

The phone buzzed again. The messages and calls had slowed down. Hopefully by the day after Christmas he will have officially moved on. That would make sense. He would want to keep the possibility open until Christmas and then when it was official for everyone else to know he would move on. Move on. Her chest tightened again. The Tums sat on the maroon counter in her dad's kitchen. The bottle was half empty. She would get him some more before she left. Misery bubbled inside her stomach. She had completely screwed herself. Not only did she leave the love of her life, she ruined things with the network. They were not exactly keen on her need for a personal moment to deal with a death in the family. Alex hadn't gone into details but they were not exactly supportive. Her fifteen minutes of fame was in a swirl to the end of the hour glass of her time to be on-air. This had been mentioned more than once in the difficult phone conversation. Alex had let a few sniffles slip through despite her desire to be a hundred percent professional.

The death was true. It was a death. Maybe not of a person but it was the death of a relationship and hopes of pure happiness. She had that, real happiness. And love, it was like he really loved her. But she couldn't get past the past. It was too much and the Tums were not the cure. The plate of Christmas cookies in front of her weren't, either. She needed to get them out of sight. If she came to in the morning and hoped to pursue the on-air route, she was going to need to be less cookies and more smiles. Air escaped from her lungs. *Smiles.* Alex shook her head. *No. Don't go there. Be strong. Take ownership and handle the situation.*

"Dad, do you want any more of the Christmas cookies?"

Her dad looked back from his recliner in the den. "No, but don't forget to leave some out for Santa." The sides of his mouth pulled up. It was a rare scene. He still wanted to pretend with her about Santa. They never really had the talk and Alex figured it was probably something that he held onto like her mom's memory.

At least that fantasy had always been real. Alex put the cookies in the tin and pushed them back into the cupboard. There. Perfect. She was always good at compartmentalizing. Everything. Job. School. Family. Love life. She laughed. What love life? Everyone had always been just a number or a name, something that looked good on paper but didn't make sense in the flesh. Nothing made sense except him.

Alex scrolled through her phone. There were several emails from the Network. It was Christmas Eve, and she was technically dealing with a death. Work could wait. Her heart needed to heal. If that was possible. Alex switched to the Socials. The last update from Cane was two days ago. It was a picture from the field aimed at the fans.

"All for you."

That was the text. Fans reshared it over and over again. They thought the message was for them. And maybe it was. But something about it, made it seem like it was for her. It was the only post of the stands he had ever done. Usually, his posts were of his muscles or the football team. Gym workouts or some delicious incredibly calorie heavy food he was about to eat. But this photo was of the stands. Not just any part of the stands. But where the reporters sat. That's what made Alex think it was for her. Her heart burned. She grabbed for the Tums and let the malty flavor crush inside of her mouth. They were so gross.

It was Christmas Eve. He had tried to call and she let him go to voicemail. Not just let, she hit the button to send him directly there. The idea of him being on the other end of the phone and the vibration of the possibility that she knew was gone was too much to watch. She had to put him in the box of no returns. No more what-could-have-been. She had sealed the end on it and them. It hurt too much. The idea of them and the idea that it wasn't real. How could he really not remember her? In college, she figured he changed his mind about the picnic and pretended he hadn't just spent the night before with her. Like next level gaslighting. It was so surreal. She had contemplated the possibility of changing her major to psychology to really uncover what had happened.

The illusion of a great night with her crush that was wiped away by rejection and a distortion to her memory. That semester was hard to process. Book after book she read. Therapy. The gym. Alex had tried everything to solve the mystery of Cane.

When the opportunity to interview him in the locker room was offered Alex was sure he had remembered her at that point. She had decided the locker room location was a precursor from Cane to let her know he did remember her. Why else would he invite her to the locker room? But she was wrong again. So very wrong.

GIA STONE

CHAPTER TWENTY-TWO

Cane held his breath before he knocked on the door. He pulled on his collar. It should not be this hot in December. What was he going to say to her? He had had three hours to think about it and he still didn't have a clue. *Sorry? I'm an idiot? Take me back? Love me.*

No one answered the door. Shit. Were they not there? Where was she? Panic squeezed the air from his lungs. *Come on, Alex.* Cane pounded on the door. He had to see her. He was sure she was here. If he had to tear down the door-he might do it. Cane shook his head. No, he wouldn't do that. He was not going to cause damage to property. The only thing he needed to tear down was the wall that Alex had built up around her heart. He raised his fist again to knock.

"Cane?" Alex's dad asked when he opened the door.

Cane unclenched his fist and reached out to shake hands. "Sorry, Mark. I know it's late. I have been trying to get a hold of Alex for the last two weeks. She isn't answering my calls. I need to talk to her." He didn't break eye contact. Man to man. He had to face her father first.

Mark let out a stream of air. "I don't want her crying anymore. I don't know what happened with you two but if you hurt her—" He poked Cane's chest. The pressure of his index finger was more than any coach had ever given him. Even when he made a bad play. Mark was serious. Cane understood.

"No. I would never hurt Alex, not on purpose. I just need to talk to her." He pulled his hands up as if to show he was only there with good intentions.

Eventually Mark nodded. "Alexandra, Santa came early."

Alex came to the door. Her hair was pulled into a ponytail. She was wearing her glasses, the ones she wore when she read, and blue fleece pajamas with a gingerbread man print. Her mouth fell open and her eyes widened.

"Hi," was all Cane could manage to say.

"Hi," she whispered.

"Well, I'm going to call it a day. Night Alexandra, I love you." Mark kissed Alex on the cheek before he turned to Cane with a warning look.

"Alex," Cane began when Mark had left. Shit! He had no idea what to say. His mind was blank. He just wanted to grab her and kiss her and never let her go. He ran a hand through his cropped hair. "Can I come in? It's kind of cold." It wasn't cold, he was burning up but he wanted to be inside where Alex couldn't slam the door on him. Cold was the best he could come up with. The only cold was the distance between them. It had been like he was on an Antarctic cruise all alone. Like a sad penguin that had been left by its flock of family.

Alex nodded. She moved to the side to allow him in. Her dad's house was huge, as big as his. But this house was a sea of maroon. No denying they were in OU territory. He had lost every single game to OU in college. This was not a good place to have confidence and no home field advantage. *Get your head in the game, Cane.* He took in a deep breath. *Focus.*

"Why are you here?" Alex's eyes were wide with confusion.

"Because you're here, Alex. Wherever you are is where I want to be. I need you. I love you but it is more than that.

So much more. I need you. I didn't even know I needed you but I do. I'm sorry. I am so sorry that I was an ass. I wish it had been different. I wish I would have remembered you. I wish I remembered the first night we were together. I wish that was our anniversary. I wish that I could tell our kids that I met their mama in college and loved her every day since. But I can't because I am an idiot, which you already knew. I am a complete fucking moron. I had a chance with you and I fucked it up. I can't even remember. I am so sorry for that. I will be sorry for that until the day I die but I will make up for it if you let me. Please, Alex. Let me make it up to you. I need you."

Alex swallowed. "Oh Cane, I missed you." She wiped her eyes with the back of her hands.

"Stop running, Alex. I love you." Cane lowered to the ground.

"What are you doing?"

"I think it's obvious. I'm taking a knee. I said I would only do it once. But I will do it every day until you say yes. Marry me, Alex."

Alex leaned down and kissed him. "Are you sure?"

Cane blinked. "Did you just ask me if I am sure I want to marry you? Do you think I'm going to change my mind? Is that it? Alex, I will love you for the rest of my life. You're it. You're mine. I don't want anyone else. Ever. Just you and me."

"And our four babies. Katrina and the three boys we haven't named yet." The corners of Alex's mouth pulled into a smile.

"And our four babies. So will you marry me?"

"Well, I don't want our children to be some sort of tabloid story so…"

"I need to hear a yes. It has been a long day and a shitty couple of weeks. I really need to lock this down."

"Lock it down? That's not very romantic. Do you want to borrow my thesaurus? My fiancé gave it to me."

Cane sighed in exasperation. "You still haven't said yes."

"The yes was implied." Alex giggled.

"We're going to have to edit this part from our official story. The part where you are awkward."

Alex took his face in her hands. "Yes. Yes, Corn Fed. I will marry you and have your freakishly large children."

Relief washed over him. She said yes. She said yes! "We will make this work. We can commute. We will have so many frequent flier miles between us. And when I miss you, I will just have to turn on ESPN. We will make this work."

Alex shook her head. "I didn't take the job."

"What?"

"I couldn't. Texas is my home. I am a sideline reporter. That's what I love. And I don't want to work anywhere where I need to starve myself to fit in. Me and my butt are meant to be in Houston." Alex turned and patted her bottom. "Didn't you notice your friend is back?"

Cane stood up and pulled Alex against him. He cupped her backside with both hands. "Not quite back but we can work on it. When the season is over, we will eat cheesecake and watch *The Vampire Diaries*."

Alex shook her head. "Nope, you're not ruining the Salvatore brothers for me. We can eat cheesecake at Perry's but I'm saving *Vampire Diaries* for Vanessa."

"Probably a good idea. Oh dang, I almost forgot the ring. Edit that part of the story, too. We need to write down our official story. You're a good writer. I'll let you handle that." Cane pulled out the light blue box and slid the diamond onto Alex's finger.

"I'm engaged," Alex said in disbelief. She held up her hand and gave her best broadcaster smile. "Take a picture, Corn Fed. This is going on Twitter. Your fangirls need to know it's time to step off."

Cane pulled out his phone and snapped a picture. "I am tagging you in this too, so be prepared for your notification to go crazy. Oh, that's right; you turned off your phone. I almost forgot. Merry Christmas. This is for our first born." Cane pulled the orange onesie out of his coat pocket.

Alex's smile stretched wide across her face, even bigger than her broadcaster smile. "Follow me, Corn Fed. I need to show you something." Alex took his hand and led him upstairs and down a long hallway to her bedroom. "I bought this after Thanksgiving. Great minds and all that." Alex handed him a navy bag tied with a red bow. Inside there was the tiniest Texans jersey Cane had ever seen.

"Turn it over," Alex said. On the back Clayburn was written in shiny black letters.

"I love it. My wife and my baby will wear my jersey."

Alex stood on her tiptoes and kissed him. Instantly he was hard. It had been too long. "Sweetheart, please forgive this performance. Next time I will bring it. But this time I just need to be inside you. Next time will be all about you. I promise."

"Corn Fed, It's like you've never met me. You know I am going to finish before you no matter how fast you go."

Cane threw his coat on the floor and reached for his zipper. "Damn woman, you're sexy. And you're mine. You might want to get your stopwatch out because this is going to be a record performance for both of us." Cane lowered them both to the bed. "I love you, Alex."

"I love you, too. But let's save the talking for the cuddle time." Alex smiled as she pulled his head down for a kiss.

The End

AUTHOR'S NOTE

Thank you for reading Alex and Cane's story. I love a second chance at romance story, but that wasn't really the case for Alex and Cane. They were more of enemies turned lovers, with a string theory concept.

Thank you for reading and purchasing this book. If you enjoyed it, please consider leaving a review or recommending to a friend.

Thank you to Katie for a million discussions about this book.

Thank you to Melissa Keir for getting Her Fake Blitz over the goal line.

Thank you to my editor Toni for coaching me into bringing the best from Alex and Cane.

Thank you to Emily's Design for a fantastic cover.

Thank you to my friend Vanessa for countless chats.

Thank you to my mom for being so supportive.

Thank you to my boys, for always making me smile.

Thank you to Allen, for the legal insight and love.

Here's a Sneak Peek at the First Book in the Houston Heights Series...

Sunset on Us

Every song was about him, except one.
Are broken promises worse than unspoken truths?

Cheyenne Ford left the small-town life of Cut and Shoot, with no intention to return. Ever. The pieces of broken gravel that flicked from her tires were not the only things she ran over with her exit.

Ten years later and still the sight of her bright red hair tore into Colt Clayburne's soul. He was not going to let her leave him again. He wouldn't be another song for her next album. Colt promised himself he wouldn't tend to a broken heart again.

Broken hearts can mend, but painful secrets are not the same as broken promises.

SUNSET ON US is a second chance romance filled with a secretive past, broken hearts, and songs that made Cheyenne Ford a household name in the Country Music circuit. Fans of Tessa Bailey and Carly Phillips' romances will love the emotional journey of Cheyenne Ford as she strives to do the right thing, even if it means walking away from the only thing she loved.

EXCERPT:

Her chest was like a fire with singed skin that traced around her lungs. She could breathe once they were out of the parking lot.

"I'm concerned about the concert," Jamison said, his eyes focused on the road.

Cheyenne jerked her head back. Jamison was never concerned with things. Or if he was, he wouldn't let on. And definitely, not to Cheyenne.

"About what?" Cheyenne glared at Jamison's biceps. They bulged through his shirt. He must have worked his upper body today. Cheyenne let her eyes run up to his neck. His jugular vein was in full pulsation mode. This was not good.

"Security. We need to have more people. The Houston crowd can get a little out of hand. Your last album crossed over into the pop market, and that brings a mix of characters." He merged onto the highway as if he was in a getaway car. No traffic laws were broken, but his moves were not his standard smooth disposition.

"Was there another letter?" The hairs along the back of her neck pricked up. It had been at least a month since the last one had been received. The police were still on the case, but Cheyenne had her doubts about what that meant. So far nothing had happened, but that didn't stop the visual of the words that flashed through her mind. Jamison had tried to keep it from her, and would have been successful had Katie not seen it in the mailbag and shown it to her. They'd both screamed. It was so nasty. Jamison had run into the room, furious. This was the third letter. The other two had already been handed over to the police.

"I want to up the security."

Cheyenne's chest tightened. "Was it like the other one?"

Available Now in Ebook and Print

ABOUT THE AUTHOR

Gia Stone is an author of steamy romances. Faulted characters, misguided motives, and misconnections are at the heart of her stories. She loves to collect passport stamps, savory memories, and race medals.

Gia's favorite quote is "The gem cannot be polished without friction, nor a person perfected without trials."

www.ingramcontent.com/pod-product-compliance
Lightning Source LLC
Chambersburg PA
CBHW022139240626
47153CB00007B/2428